Raven licked her lips.

The mood had certainly shifted in here, as if the cold air from outside had seeped in through the window. It suited her. Guilt piled upon guilt didn't engender lustful thoughts.

But the slabs of hard muscle across Buzz's chest did.

"You want to join me tonight?" He patted the bed beside him.

She needed more seduction than a stark question. She'd already been feeling as if they'd been punished for their attention to each othe

"I don't think that's a great idea, Buzz—for a lot of reasons."

He shrugged. "We may have different reasons, but I agree with you." He squeezed her hand as she rose from the bed. "Get a good night's sleep."

Raven clicked the bedroom door behind her and leaned her forehead against it. A good night's sleep with peril on both sides of her?

That wasn't going to happen.

CAROL ERICSON

TOP GUN GUARDIAN

TORONTO NEW YORK LONDON
AMSTERDAM PARIS SYDNEY HAMBURG
STOCKHOLM ATHENS TOKYO MILAN MADRID
PRAGUE WARSAW BUDAPEST AUCKLAND

For Randy, my top gun neighbor.

Recycling programs
for this product may
not exist in your area.

ISBN-13: 978-0-373-74641-5

TOP GUN GUARDIAN

Copyright © 2011 by Carol Ericson

www.Harlequin.com

Printed in U.S.A.

ABOUT THE AUTHOR

Carol Ericson lives with her husband and two sons in Southern California, home of state-of-the-art cosmetic surgery, wild freeway chases, palm trees bending in the Santa Ana winds and a million amazing stories. These stories, along with hordes of virile men and feisty women, clamor for release from Carol's head. It makes for some interesting headaches until she sets them free to fulfill their destinies and her readers' fantasies. To find out more about Carol, her books and her strange headaches, please visit her website at www.carolericson.com, "where romance flirts with danger."

Books by Carol Ericson

HARLEQUIN INTRIGUE
1034—THE STRANGER AND I
1079—A DOCTOR-NURSE ENCOUNTER
1117—CIRCUMSTANTIAL MEMORIES
1184—THE SHERIFF OF SILVERHILL
1231—THE MCCLINTOCK PROPOSAL
1250—A SILVERHILL CHRISTMAS
1267—NAVY SEAL SECURITY*
1273—MOUNTAIN RANGER RECON*
1320—TOP GUN GUARDIAN*

*BROTHERS IN ARMS

CAST OF CHARACTERS

Raven Pierre—Raven is a big-city girl. When the young daughter of an imperiled African president lands in her lap and her ex-fiancé jumps in to protect them, her big-city veneer begins to crack and her heart shows signs of melting.

Bryan "Buzz" Richardson—A former member of the covert ops team Prospero, Buzz swoops in to guard a girl targeted by terrorists, hoping his protection of her gets him closer to finding missing Prospero member Jack Coburn. The fact that his assignment also gets him closer to his ex-fiancée is icing on the cake.

Malika Okeke—She forms a bond with Raven after Raven saves her life, but now the girl's attachment to her savior might just get them both killed.

President Okeke—The newly elected president of a fledgling African country, the president has ties in his past to terrorists.

Rodeo Clown—Clowns are supposed to be funny, but Raven isn't laughing at the mysterious rodeo clown who shows up again and again.

Lance Cooper—He blames Buzz for his brother's death in a plane crash.

Jeb Russell—A CIA agent who wants Malika, and may be willing to take her by force.

Farouk—Prospero's former nemesis has expanded his business model and taken his terror worldwide.

Colonel Scripps—Prospero's coordinator, the Colonel knows he can summon all of the former team members with one call.

Jack Coburn—The former leader of Prospero and current hostage negotiator has run into a little trouble.

Prologue

He stared into the boy's face, searching for arti-fice...or danger. The boy blinked several times and hunched his shoulders.

He loosened his grip on the youth, but kept his muscles coiled and ready in case the kid ran off. He couldn't allow him to escape.

This scruffy street urchin just might hold the key to his identity.

He leaned close to the boy's ear and whispered, "Do you know me?"

A big grin split the urchin's brown face and then melted away as he gazed into the eyes of his captor. "Of course I know you, Mr. Jack. It is me, Yasir."

"Yasir?" Despite the chill in the morning air, he wiped a bead of sweat from beneath his head-dress. "And my name is Jack?"

The boy nodded, his black brows meeting over his nose. "You do not know your name? What happened to you, Mr. Jack? I do not see you for a week."

Jack jerked his thumb over his left shoulder. "See that mountain range back there? I woke up on a rock this morning with no memory."

Yasir's mouth dropped open, his missing teeth giving him the look of a jack-o'-lantern. He jabbed a finger into Jack's ribs where a splotch of blood stained his grubby shirt. "Did they get you, Mr. Jack?"

A tingle of fear climbed its way up Jack's back and he clenched his muscles to ward it off. "Who are *they,* Yasir? What am I? What am I doing here? Where's here?"

The kid held up his callused hands. "Okey-dokey, Mr. Jack. We go to your place. I bring you food."

Jack tensed. Could this be a trap? Did he really have a home in this teeming village of goat herders and traders and farmers?

He looked into the boy's earnest brown eyes. Did he have a choice right now?

"Okey-dokey, Yasir. I'll follow you."

Keeping his head bowed, Jack trailed after Yasir, weaving his way through the press of people. Except for a few nods directed at Yasir, nobody halted their progress through the streets of the village. Nobody attacked him.

Glancing both ways, Yasir darted into an alley

and Jack slipped in behind him. A few doorways into the pungent, narrow space, Yasir ducked into a small room, pulling Jack in behind him.

Jack blinked, adjusting his eyes to the gloom. An old man dozed in a chair, and Yasir tiptoed past him. He flicked aside a coarse blanket hanging from the ceiling and waved Jack through with one hand.

Licking his dry lips, Jack sidled through the opening and crept into a room even smaller than the adjoining one. His gaze flicked across the cot in the corner, a low table with a guttered candle on top of it and a few makeshift shelves holding books—lots of books.

A flicker of recognition flitted across his brain, and he dropped to his knees on the dirt floor to squint at the titles. Yasir nudged him in the back, and Jack spun around with his hands clenched.

"Jumpy, Mr. Jack." With two steps, Yasir crossed the small space and kicked a black duffel bag at the foot of the cot. "This is yours. You take everywhere."

Crawling to the cot, Jack snagged the strap of the duffel bag and dragged it between his legs as he perched on the edge of the crude bed. He yanked at the zipper and the sides of the bag gaped open.

Yasir scraped a match against the earthen wall of the room. Jack's nostrils twitched at the smell of sulfur. Yasir lit the candle on the table and a soft yellow glow illuminated the small, dank space.

Grabbing the edges of the bag, Jack peeled it open. His brows shot up as his fingers traced the bundles of cash neatly stashed in the bag. Dozens of passports littered the top of the money stacks, and a gun was tucked in the corner of the bag.

His gaze darted toward Yasir's face, waxy in the candlelight, but displaying no surprise at the contents of the bag. Jack dug his hands into the pile of passports and let them slide through his fingers. "Why is this here? Why didn't you steal the money when I disappeared?"

A crooked smile played across the boy's face. "What I do with all that money in my Afghan village, Mr. Jack? And if I take—" he shrugged his narrow shoulders "—you hunt me down and kill me."

Jack coughed, a sour knot forming in his belly. Is that what he was? Would he kill a boy for stealing money?

"I doubt that, Yasir." He grabbed one of the passports and flipped it open—John Coughlin, citizen of the U.K. He scooped up another: Jacques Durand, citizen of France. He nabbed the American passport: Jack Wilson. Was he Jack Wilson? He studied the picture of the man with the long blond hair, a moustache and glasses.

He knew he didn't wear glasses and he didn't have a moustache…at least not yet. "Yasir, is there a mirror in here?"

"That is not you, Mr. Jack. You Mr. Jack Coburn and you American spy." Yasir groped beneath the cot and dragged out a bin filled with shaving supplies, including a dingy mirror.

A spy, huh? Jack held the mirror in front of him and slid the headdress from his head. Long hair, but black. No glasses. No moustache. Dark eyes, hard eyes.

He peered at the passport photo again, detecting blue eyes behind the glasses. How the hell was he going to get out of this country? Because he'd decided that's exactly what he had to do.

And then Yasir read his mind, his much damaged mind.

"Disguises, Mr. Jack." Yasir patted the side pockets of the duffel bag.

Jack unzipped one side and dipped his hand inside the compartment. He pulled out wigs, facial hair, containers of contact lenses. Poking around the pocket on the other side, he found more of the same. All of these costume pieces most likely matched the photos on the myriad passports spilling out of the duffel bag.

Now he had the means to get out of here and away from the people who'd left him on that mountainside. Then what? Should he seek an

American embassy? Get back to the States and turn himself in to some agency there?

Leaving the money in the bag, Jack dumped the remaining contents on the floor and sifted through it. Between two fingers, he pinched a white sheet of paper folded in two. He shook the dirt from it and unfolded it, flattening the paper on his knee. It was a brief note: *Thank you for your help, Mr. Coburn, and thank you for your discretion. If you bring Gabriel home safely, I'll have another million waiting for you. Warm regards and Godspeed, Lola Famosa.*

An address in Miami followed the flowery signature.

Jack narrowed his eyes as the candle sputtered. He didn't know the identity of Gabriel or the condition of his safety, but he now knew where to start to figure out his own identity.

He was going to pay a visit to Ms. Lola Famosa of Miami.

Chapter One

Raven Pierre eyed the small girl clutching the baby doll in one grubby hand and growled in the back of her throat. It figured her supervisor, Walter, would give her kid duty just because she happened to be the only female translator on this job.

She didn't even like kids.

Why did the president of the newly formed African nation Burumanda bring his daughter to the United Nations for his first address anyway? The General Assembly was no place for kids. Even Raven knew that.

Raven's gaze shifted back to the little girl whose liquid brown eyes wandered between the closed-circuit TV screen and the impassive Secret Service agent parked in the chair across from her, sipping a soda. The girl's small tongue darted from her mouth and swept across her lips.

Was the kid allowed to drink soda?

Raven pointed to the can clutched in the agent's

hand and said in the girl's native dialect, "Do you want one?"

The girl nodded, her pigtails bobbing vigorously. "My name is Malika. What is your name?"

Raven raised her brows. Sounded like pretty good English to her. Maybe Malika, who looked maybe eight, didn't even need a translator. "My name is Raven. Your English is good."

Malika snapped her fingers. "English is easy language. Official language of Burumanda now. Your Chichewa—" she wrinkled her nose "—is fine."

Just *fine?* Raven narrowed her eyes. Maybe Malika was eighteen instead of eight. Raven never could guess kids' ages anyway. "Do you want a soda? I can ask one of your guards out front to bring us a couple."

As Raven pushed back her chair, the agent reached for his own can and knocked it to the floor where it fizzled and bubbled.

Raven snorted. "Smooth move, Garrett."

The agent slumped forward, banging his head on the table. With her heart thumping, Raven stumbled to his side. She clutched his forearm through the dark material of his suit jacket. "Garrett?"

Was he fooling around? Raven swallowed hard. Secret Service agents didn't fool around, especially Garrett Hansen.

"Is he sick?" Malika hugged her doll to her chest, her eyes round with fear.

Raven's gut twisted. Malika had lost her mother in the war to establish Burumanda. The kid had witnessed a lot of death and destruction in her short lifetime.

Death? Garrett had probably just eaten something that didn't agree with him.

Raven slid her hand to his wrist, where she felt a pulse pumping away. "Garrett, are you okay?"

She patted his clammy cheek and his head rolled to the side, his mouth gaping open. With shaky fingers, Raven fumbled in the pocket of her slacks for her cell phone. Should she call 911, Walter, the Secret Service?

Closing her eyes, she blew out a breath. She'd start with the bodyguards standing sentry on the other side of the doorway.

She tripped to the door of the anteroom and swung it open. The two burly Burumandan guards were carbon copies of Garrett, slumped sideways in their chairs.

Adrenaline zinged through Raven's system and she backpedaled away from the empty hallway leading toward the General Assembly. Unless the three men had all eaten the same lunch, this was no coincidence.

Noise from the closed-circuit TV erupted, and

Raven spun around to see Malika clap one hand over her mouth. *Gunfire.*

"They are shooting at my father."

Raven peered at the screen and the frantic figures darting around the General Assembly. She glanced at the doorway gaping open, and clenched her jaw. Shots fired in the General Assembly at President Okeke. His daughter's bodyguards passed out cold. She loved shoes but didn't plan to stick around and wait for the third one to drop.

Raven strode back toward the door, slammed it shut and locked it. Crouching next to the inert form of Garrett, she slipped her hand inside his jacket. She lifted the gun from his shoulder holster and released the safety. She gave silent thanks to her ex-fiancé and his buddies from the covert ops team, Prospero, for teaching her how to shoot. She'd been great at target practice, but she'd never had to shoot at a moving target and never once to save her life…or someone else's.

A cacophony of voices and a stampede of footsteps echoed on the other side of the door. Raven froze, her gaze glued to the slowly turning door handle. Finding it locked, somebody rapped on the door. With what sounded like the butt of a gun.

At this point, she had no idea whom to trust. She swept her handbag from the back of the chair.

She nudged Malika, rooted in front of the TV, her doll dangling from her fingers. "Let's go. And get a grip on that doll."

Malika whimpered and folded her arms across her belly, shooting a glance at the door, still under assault from someone on the other side.

"Don't worry. We're not going that way. Why do you think they put you in here in the first place?"

Raven crept across the room and pressed a panel with her palm. She felt the spring give beneath her hand and she slid the panel to the side, where an opening yawned in the wall. She turned and gestured at Malika.

The girl tiptoed toward the wall and jumped at a particularly loud thump on the door. Raven grabbed her arm and pulled her through the opening. She slid the panel back into place and tucked Malika behind her. Pressing her ear against the wall, she put a finger to her lips.

Malika wrapped one arm around Raven's waist and trembled against her back. Raven straightened her spine to give them both a little confidence.

The door on the other side burst open with the sound of splintering wood. Raven held her breath as the blood pounded in her ears. *Friend or foe?*

"Where are they? I thought you said they were in here."

Raven flinched at the sound of a sickening thud of flesh against hard wood. Garrett's head?

"Obviously they were in here. That's why he's here."

Accents. One German, one French.

"Maybe they're still here."

Malika's grip tightened, squeezing the breath from Raven.

"We don't have time to search. Once the pandemonium subsides and they try to raise their comrade here on his radio, they'll be crawling all over the place."

"We can't afford not to search. We need the girl."

With shaky hands, Raven slipped her high heels from her feet. She tapped Malika on the head with the toe of one shoe and pointed toward the set of stairs that disappeared into the darkness.

If the two men started banging around out there, Raven had no intention of waiting until they discovered the hollow cavity in the wall. She didn't have a clue as to the meaning of this assault, but she knew danger when it stared her in the face. Two years working as a translator with Prospero in the Middle East had taught her that.

She laced her fingers with Malika's and guided her down the steps. She had to hand it to the little girl. The minute Raven had given the command to go, Malika had performed like a champ—no tears, no tantrums, just flight.

They crept down the stairs and reached a door. "Hold it." Raven held up her hand. Turning the tarnished metal handle, she eased open the door and peeked into the deserted hallway. She crooked her finger at Malika to follow and then tiptoed into the open space, feeling exposed and vulnerable.

Raven hated feeling vulnerable.

Her grip on Garrett's gun tightened as she pulled Malika close to her side. They sidled along the wall. Raven had spent plenty of time in this building and knew exactly where they were. She also knew the location of a janitor's closet nearby.

She had the overwhelming sense that she needed to keep Malika under wraps. Anyone could be out there now. She didn't even know if President Okeke was dead or alive.

Reaching the closet door, Raven pulled it open and shoved Malika inside the small space crowded with brooms, mops and buckets.

Raven whispered. "We're going to stay here for a while until I can figure out what's going on."

In the darkness, Malika scooched in closer to Raven, who could feel the trembling of the small girl's body. She slipped an arm around Malika and squeezed her shoulder. "It's going to be okay. Do you understand?"

Malika nodded, tickling Raven's chin with her hair. Then she slipped her sticky hand in Raven's. Why did kids always have dirty hands? Raven curled her fingers around Malika's.

Despite the recent turn of events, maybe President Okeke had the right idea bringing his daughter along. It beat stashing her with some nanny or shoving her into some boarding school. Raven knew all about that.

She'd vowed never to do anything like that to her children. And the best guarantee against that was to skip motherhood altogether. Of course, that decision had cost her Buzz, her ex-fiancé. Second time she'd thought of Buzz today, not that she didn't think of him every week, or dream about him, or...

Must be all the high-octane excitement.

"Now that we're in a safe place, I'm going to get us some help." Raven slipped her cell phone out of her pocket where she'd dropped it after discovering the comatose bodyguards. Walter should know the status of events. She called him, only to have her cell phone inform her that a closet in the middle of the U.N. was no place to get reception.

Malika tapped the phone. "Help?"

"Not yet. We'll stay here for a little while longer. Police and security should have this building secured shortly, and then we can just walk out." Raven patted her oversized handbag, where she'd stashed Garrett's weapon. "Besides, I have protection."

Malika emitted a puff of air from her lips. "My mother had a gun, too."

A knot tightened in Raven's chest. This little girl had been through too much already. When would it end? Raven's own childhood had been no picnic, but privilege, wealth and distant parents couldn't compare to revolution, gunfire and death.

"D-did you see it happen?" Raven bit her lip as Malika stiffened beside her. Any idiot knew you didn't ask a child questions like that. You should change the subject, pretend it never happened, stuff down those feelings.

Raven should know better. That's how every adult had treated her as a child, even after her little brother had drowned in the family pool.

Malika drew in a noisy, wet breath. "Yes. The rebels broke into our home. They got past our security forces. My mother had her gun—" Malika lifted her shoulder "—but they got her first."

"I'm sorry, Malika. That must have been...horrible." What an inadequate word. The kid must think she's some kind of monster for asking her to dredge up that moment.

Malika increased the pressure of her fingers

around Raven's hand. "My father never asked me about it."

Raven glanced down, trying to discern the expression on Malika's face in the dark. Maybe Raven hadn't been crazy for wanting to talk about her brother, Jace, after he'd died. But nobody would allow her to talk about him. Instead they'd politely avoided the topic and studied Raven's every word and expression for signs of trauma. Her parents were big on opening up…to a bevy of therapists, anyway.

A footstep fell in the hallway, and Raven's body jerked.

Malika pressed her head against her knees, her entire frame tensing. Raven slipped her hand into her handbag and withdrew the gun. She released the safety and pointed it toward the closet door. She didn't plan to go down without a fight. And she didn't plan on allowing anyone to snatch this brave girl beside her.

A door opened and closed, and Malika rolled her head to the side, resting her cheek on Raven's knee. "They are coming. They always come."

A twist of fear spiraled up Raven's spine and she shook it off. No time to panic. It could be the police or U.N. security or even Burumandan security forces.

Yeah, like the ones who killed Malika's mother?

A bead of sweat rolled along her hairline. With

her finger poised on the trigger of the gun, Raven braced her stockinged feet against the door. She knew the door swung outward, giving her an advantage over their stealthy attacker. She could hit him with the door first...and then the bullet if it became necessary.

Then they'd just have to chance it and run helter-skelter out of the building, throwing themselves on the mercy of the first uniformed person they encountered.

Raven coiled her muscles as the footsteps drew nearer. Target practice had nothing on real-world situations.

Another door snapped shut. Click, click. Dull clicks, not women's high heels but a man's dress shoes or some kind of heavy heels. Not the soft soles of a security guard or cop. Secret Service?

Her legs ached with tension, trembling with the effort to stay poised for action. Click, click. Pause. The handle of the door turned.

Raven flattened her feet against the door and coiled her thigh muscles. A slice of light appeared, and she shoved her legs forward. The door hit resistance. Raven sprang to her feet and charged out of the closet, clutching the gun in front of her.

A man in a dark suit staggered back, cursing and reaching beneath his jacket.

Raven steadied her weapon and took up a

shooting stance, just like Buzz had taught her. "Don't move or I'll blow a hole in your gut."

The man dropped his hands and jerked his head up. A slow smile spread across his handsome face.

"If it isn't Raven Pierre—city girl turned… gun-totin' vigilante. And you already blew a hole in my gut, girl."

Raven choked as she scanned the tall figure in front of her dressed in a tailored suit and… cowboy boots. Her gaze traveled back up, all six feet three inches, until she met the blue eyes, brimming with laughter, of her ex-fiancé and former weapons instructor, Buzz Richardson.

Chapter Two

Damn, his ex-fiancée looked better than ever with her black hair slightly askew, her expensive silk suit wrinkled and a Colt .45 clutched in her manicured hands.

But what the hell was she doing hiding in a closet?

"What are you doing in there? U.N. security already has the two shooters in custody, or at least one's in custody. The other's dead. They nailed the two guys right in the General Assembly."

The news did nothing to unfurl the frown creasing her beautiful features. Her hand tightened on the weapon as she narrowed her dark eyes. "They didn't nail all of them."

His pulse ticked up several notches. "What are you talking about? You weren't even with the Burumandan contingent."

"I was with one part of that contingent. One very important part." She stepped to the side and swung open the closet door behind her.

Buzz raised his brows at the girl huddled in the closet, her chin balanced on her knees. President Okeke's daughter. He should have figured Raven's boss had assigned her to the First Daughter. Security was going nuts looking for the girl after finding her bodyguards and the Secret Service agent conked out in the anteroom where she'd been stashed.

Still didn't explain why Raven had been ensconced in a dark closet with the girl. Raven didn't even like kids. He knew all about that firsthand.

Buzz smiled and waved at the girl. "How you doin', sweetheart? Excitement's all over. Your daddy's A-OK."

Her big brown eyes got bigger. She dropped her gaze to his boots and then sent a beseeching look toward Raven.

"Does she speak English?"

Raven snorted and finally lowered her weapon. "She speaks better English than you, Buzz."

Extending a hand to the girl, she said, "It's all right, Malika. I know this man. He's…safe."

Buzz cocked an eyebrow at Raven. She'd never called him *safe* before.

As the girl scrambled out of the closet and grabbed Raven's hand, Buzz folded his arms and squared his shoulders. "What did you mean about not nailing all of them?"

"When Garrett and then the bodyguards lost consciousness and we saw the shooting erupt on the closed-circuit TV, I didn't want to take any chances." She dipped into the closet, grabbed her handbag and tucked the gun away in it. "I mean, why incapacitate Malika's security if you're just shooting at President Okeke?"

Buzz's mouth went dry and he ran his tongue along his teeth. "Your time with Prospero paid off. Go on."

"So I locked the door of the anteroom, grabbed Garrett's gun and headed for the secret exit."

"There's a secret exit in the anteroom?"

She nodded, and her dark hair swept across one shoulder. "I know all the ins and outs in this building."

"And the secret exit led you here?"

"Not before I heard two men in the anteroom desperate to find the president's daughter." Raven rested a hand on the girl's shoulder.

Buzz tightened his jaw. President Okeke had been whisked away to a secure hotel room, frantic over his daughter's disappearance. Shortly after the shooting, the CIA had gotten word that rebel forces had attacked the capital of Burumanda. And now the First Daughter was in danger.

"We need to keep her safe." He crouched in front of the girl. "What's your name, darlin'?"

Again, her gaze slid to Raven, who inclined her head.

"Malika."

"A lot of people are very worried about you, Malika, including your daddy. But we're going to take good care of you."

The girl inched closer to Raven and clutched her hand, still resting on Malika's shoulder. Must have been the fear that had drawn these two together. He'd never seen Raven close to a child before.

He liked it.

"What next, Buzz? Are we going to bring Malika to her father?"

"Not so fast, Raven." He ran a finger along the seam of his lips. Truth was President Okeke didn't want his daughter anywhere near him. He didn't want his proximity to put her in danger. And neither one of them could go home right now with trouble brewing.

Raven dug into her suitcase-sized handbag and pulled out a pair of shoes—high heels with lethal-looking points on the ends. She slipped her feet into them and grew four inches in stature. "What is your involvement, anyway? I thought you'd retired from Prospero and were flying the friendly skies for a living. What are you doing here?"

"Special assignment." A special assignment that had everything to do with Prospero. Jack

Coburn, the former team leader of Prospero, was missing and his disappearance had been linked to the upheaval in Burumanda. Buzz needed to stay involved in this investigation and follow the trail that had begun with his former Prospero team members, Riley Hammond and Ian Dempsey.

"So I repeat—" Raven tugged at the hem of her jacket "—what next?"

Buzz studied the toes of his boots. "We're going to let President Okeke know his daughter is safe and take our cue from him."

"Hold it. Put your hands out where I can see them."

Buzz raised his head to see two cops at the end of the hallway…both pointing guns. He held his hands out in front of him and told Raven to do the same.

Raven coughed as she shook her hand loose from Malika's. "Can't they see we have a child here? They shouldn't be pointing their weapons at us."

Buzz murmured under his breath. "Unless they think we're in the process of kidnapping her."

Raven called out to the approaching cops. "This is President Okeke's daughter. I'm a U.N. translator. I was with her when the shots were fired in the General Assembly."

One of the cops spoke into the radio on his

shoulder. Then he tightened the grip on his gun.
"Until we can verify that, get on the ground."

As Raven grumbled about the general condition of her silk suit and dropped to her knees, Malika screamed and threw her arms around Raven's waist.

"Do not hurt Raven."

Buzz's eyes nearly popped out of his skull. Raven and this little girl had sure forged a bond over the past hour.

And he had every intention of using it to his advantage.

RAVEN TAPPED HER STOCKINGED feet together as she sipped a diet soda and furrowed her brow at the cartoon on TV. The cartoon hero was a sponge living underwater. How could that be funny?

Malika giggled and bounced on the bed next to Raven. "He is very funny but stupid."

Raven smiled at her. Malika hadn't wanted to leave her side ever since the cops turned them over to a phalanx of security people and eventually Malika's father at the hotel.

The president had been so relieved to see his daughter and had showered so much praise on Raven, she thought he was going to offer her a position in his new government. Or what was left of that government after the renewed rebel attacks.

Raven's gaze shifted to the closed door between the hotel suite and the conference room. High government mucky-mucks were in there now with President Okeke…and Buzz.

How had Buzz known she'd been hiding in that closet? He'd maintained that he had super-duper radar where it concerned her. She'd almost given him a big kiss, well, after she'd almost shot him. Warm relief had flooded her body when she'd looked into his baby blues. That man always could make her feel safer than an egg packed in cotton.

"See." Malika poked her in the ribs. "Very funny sponge."

"He's hilarious." Raven rolled her eyes. Holding up her soda can, she asked, "Do you want another one?"

Malika nodded and bounced on the mattress again. Raven rolled off the bed and padded to the minibar. Why not? The kid deserved a double shot of sugar and caffeine after the morning she'd had.

She handed Malika a frosty can and settled against the pillows. She'd known Prospero had disbanded and had heard that Buzz was working as a commercial airline pilot. Did he have a wife and baby to go along with his white picket fence? She hadn't noticed a wedding ring on his long, strong fingers—and she'd been looking.

Sighing, she wiggled her toes. They had gotten engaged when they were both still working with Prospero, the covert ops group headed by Jack Coburn. Jack was the one who had recruited her to translate some of their bugged conversations between terrorists.

She still couldn't figure out why she'd fallen for Buzz instead of Jack. Jack had been as commitmentphobic as she was, a loner. Maybe that was it. She would've had to try too hard to maintain any kind of relationship with Jack, while a relationship with Buzz had been inevitable from the moment they met.

Once Buzz had decided on her, there was no holding him back. With his slow Oklahoma drawl and his easy grin, he'd swept her off her feet before she even knew his true intentions. Once he had a ring on her finger, he'd revealed his plans for settling in the small Oklahoma town where he grew up and raising a passel of kids. He'd even used the word *passel*.

Raven had taken off faster than one of those jets Buzz maneuvered through the sky like a paper airplane.

The connecting door swung open, and Raven's fingers clawed into the bedspread. She still hadn't regained her composure after the wild escape at the U.N. But she always put up a good front.

President Okeke opened his arms, and Malika

hurled herself off the bed and against his chest. He smiled and winked at Raven over Malika's head. "Are you happy here with Miss Pierre?"

"Yes, she gave me soda pop and fixed my hair." Malika twirled one finger around her pigtail.

Raven had bounded off the bed and stuffed her feet into her heels when the president had entered the room with Buzz lounging against the doorjamb behind him. Her cheeks heated and she spoke in the president's dialect to restore her dignity. "I hope the soda is not a problem, Mr. President."

He waved his hands. "A small treat for a difficult morning, and please speak English. We do not want to be rude to our friend Mr. Richardson."

Friend? Raven narrowed her eyes, giving Buzz a sidelong glance. He sure had gotten chummy with the president in a short space of time. Leave it to Buzz. He could charm just about anyone into anything.

She should know.

"Are you finished in there? Have they found a safe place for you and your daughter?" Not that Raven wanted to dump Malika. The girl had grown on her...a little. But she did have a life and a fabulous apartment on the Upper East Side and even a date for dinner.

Her gaze wandered across Buzz's wide shoulders and broad chest. Her date didn't have a fraction of Buzz's mouthwatering physical attributes. But he had something Buzz lacked—a big-city, superficial nonchalance that suited Raven just fine.

President Okeke shifted his gaze to Buzz and then back to her. "We're not quite finished. We have a few more details to arrange."

Buzz stepped to the side as the door behind him nudged open. A suit stuck his head into the room. "Everything fine with your daughter, President Okeke? We'll have the two of you out of this hotel and installed in a secure location in no time at all."

The president nodded and crouched next to Malika. He whispered something in her ear in their own language, and Raven caught just one word—*safe.*

The Secret Service agent ushered President Okeke back into the conference room and held the door open for Buzz. "Are you joining us?"

The agent's clipped tone made it clear he didn't think Buzz warranted a place at the table with the Secretary of State and the other high-level security representatives.

Buzz shrugged. "You don't really need me in there. I'll hang out here and watch—" he cocked his head at the TV "—the sponge."

The agent smirked and snapped the door shut.

Buzz pressed his ear against the door for several seconds and then locked the deadbolt with a soft click. He pointed to the minibar fridge. "Can I have one of those five-dollar sodas?"

Raven frowned at the door. Did Buzz think they were in danger from anyone in that room? Not likely.

Tapping Malika on the head as she walked by, Raven said, "We've pretty much decimated the colas. Do you want a root beer?"

"Sure. Give me a root beer for the road."

Raven swiveled her head around. "For the road? Where are you going? I thought you'd want to see this thing through."

"Not just me." Buzz took two large steps to the minibar and snatched the can from Raven's slack hand. "We're all going."

"Yeah, well, once the suits in the other room find a secure location for President Okeke and Malika—" Raven slammed the door to the little fridge and pushed up to her feet "—we'll all be going. And we'd better hurry because I have a hot date."

Buzz raised one brow and snapped the lid on his can. "We're not waiting for them. We're headed for that secure location right now, the three of us."

Biting her lip, Raven shot a glance at the locked

door again. "I-is that the plan? We're going there first and then the president will follow us?"

Buzz dipped his head once and chucked Malika under the chin.

Malika had already slipped into her shoes and had grabbed her doll from the bed. She didn't seem surprised or alarmed at the news that they were leaving the hotel ahead of her father.

Raven rubbed out the furrow between her eyebrows. But why did *she* have to come along? "Buzz, are you sure I'm included in this plan?"

"Don't you want to help Malika?" His brows shot up to his hairline. "You're about the only one she trusts right now. Isn't that right, darlin'?"

Malika pinned Raven with her big brown eyes and nodded.

Raven sucked in a breath and then blew it out, rolling back her shoulders. She was not going to allow Buzz Richardson to accuse her of disliking little children…again.

She checked her Rolex. She could still meet her date on time. How long could it take to stash Malika and a few bodyguards in some safehouse?

Rubbing Malika's back, Raven said, "Of course I want to help Malika. We're a team—at least until her father takes over."

"I knew I could count on your love of children to propel you in the right direction." Buzz grabbed her handbag from the credenza and shoved it against her chest. "Let's go."

"Shouldn't we let them know we're on our way?" She jerked her thumb toward the room next door.

"They're busy." Buzz inched open the door to the suite and exchanged a few words with the Burumandan guard stationed there.

The man trailed them down the hallway to the stairwell, and then followed them down four flights of stairs. When they burst through the final fire door, Buzz guided them away from the lobby and toward a side door. The door landed them in the middle of the busy kitchen, where they darted through a maze of counters, refrigerators and vats of churning food.

When they hit the back door of the kitchen, their escort melted away and another intercepted them as they entered an alley on the side of the hotel. Their guard hustled them into a Lincoln Town Car with tinted windows.

Despite the blacked-out windows, Buzz told Raven and Malika to slouch in their seats. Raven swallowed her complaints when she noticed Malika's swift compliance. The girl had experience in this sort of subterfuge.

The car shot out of the alley and Raven whispered to Buzz. "I'm glad this guy has diplomatic immunity or they'd throw the book at him for reckless driving." The car squealed around the first corner. "And speeding."

The driver whisked the car down the FDR Drive and Raven peeked out the window. The safehouse must be outside of Manhattan. Maybe she wouldn't make it to her date on time after all.

That was probably for the best. How could she possibly concentrate on another man when she'd just spent an adrenaline-fueled day with Buzz? His larger-than-life presence eclipsed everyone. It just wasn't fair he had to come traipsing back into her life, reminding her of what she'd thrown away.

Malika had conked out and slumped to the side, resting her head against Raven's arm. A little drool had trickled from the corner of Malika's mouth onto the sleeve of Raven's suit. Raven rummaged through her bag for a tissue and dabbed the girl's lips.

Raven met Buzz's eyes above Malika's head. "What? She's drooling on my new suit."

"She really likes you." He spread his hands in front of him as if he couldn't believe it.

"Yeah, well, I saved her life back there at the U.N. What would you expect?"

He lifted one shoulder. "I would expect her to like you. Kids do."

"You're crazy. I was never around them enough for you to gauge that."

"There was Eric and Grace's boy."

Raven gave an exaggerated shiver. "You mean that horrid little monster who ran around putting tadpoles on everyone's lap?"

Buzz laughed and the sound filled the backseat of the Town Car, coaxing a grin from Raven. "Except yours."

"That's because I warned him if he came anywhere near me with a tadpole, I'd take the critter and flush him down the toilet."

"And he fell in love with you on the spot. Followed you around for the rest of the party…without his tadpoles."

"Ha! He probably just wanted to make sure I wouldn't get my hands on any of his creatures and flush 'em." Raven pressed her warm forehead against the cool window. "Where is this place?"

"We're almost there."

Several minutes later, the car exited the highway and pulled into a small parking lot next to a low-slung gray building.

Raven tapped the window. "This is a secure location? It looks like, it looks like…an airplane hangar."

The car jerked to a stop and Buzz threw open the door.

Raven clawed at the door handle, her heart pounding. Buzz. Airplanes. The two went together like…little boys and tadpoles. "Buzz! Buzz!"

She clambered out of the car. "What are we doing here?"

He dipped back into the car on the other side, and Raven ducked her head inside, too. Did he think he could avoid her that easily? They nearly banged foreheads over Malika's sleepy form.

Raven hissed. "What are you doing?"

He tucked his arms beneath Malika and slid her across the seat toward him. "I'm kidnapping President Okeke's daughter. And you're coming with me."

Chapter Three

"Bryan!"

Buzz grinned. Raven must be really mad to use his real name instead of his nickname. He had to play this right because he needed Raven for the plan to work.

He waved to the mechanic he'd called earlier. "Did you do the pre-flight? Everything ready to go?"

"You're good to go, boss." The mechanic flashed him a thumbs-up.

Clutching a drowsy Malika to his chest, Buzz strode across the tarmac to his Jetstream. Two steps up and he felt a tug at his shirt. He suppressed a grin and twisted his head over his shoulder.

Raven's dark eyes sparkled, practically shooting sparks. "Where are you taking Malika and why?"

"I'm taking her to safety."

"Are you crazy? You'll have the entire CIA,

FBI and probably the U.S. Military after you, not to mention some of those huge Burumandan security guys."

He pointed to Naru, the Burumandan driver waving on the tarmac. "You mean like him? I'm not as crazy as I look, Raven. I have President Okeke's permission to take Malika. We'd already discussed and planned it."

Her black, sculpted eyebrows collided over her nose. "But why? I thought that's what you were all figuring out in the conference room. Are you telling me President Okeke doesn't trust the United States government?"

"He trusts me more. And you."

"Me?" Raven ran a hand through her silky hair, the color of velvet midnight. "I just met the guy."

"You saved his daughter's life." Malika stirred in his arms, rubbing the back of her hand across her nose. "We can't waste any more time out here. I have to get her in the plane and get going."

Raven took a step down, one heel digging into the asphalt of the tarmac. "I can't come with you."

"President Okeke specifically requested that you accompany us. He wanted to ask you himself at the hotel, but the Secret Service agent interrupted him."

Buzz held his breath. Raven lived and breathed her career, and Buzz could imagine how she felt being relegated to babysitting duty. Now through a set of crazy circumstances, the new president of Burumanda needed her help. Buzz would have to keep pounding on that to convince her to come along.

"The president believes his daughter's safety rests with you. He never would've hatched this plan if not for his confidence in you, Raven."

She shook her head and pursed her lips. "I can't rush off and leave everything, especially for some cockamamie scheme of yours. If you're involved, trouble is not far behind. How do I even know you have President Okeke's permission to take Malika?"

"And why would I want to kidnap the president's daughter?" Of course, he didn't have to tell Raven about the link between the assassination attempt on President Okeke and Jack Coburn's disappearance. That wouldn't convince her of anything except his insanity.

Raven's right foot joined her left foot firmly on the ground. "I can't do it, Buzz. You're on your own."

Buzz clenched his jaw. That's not the first time she'd said those words to him.

Malika squirmed in his arms, lifting her head from his shoulder. "Raven?"

"You're going to be fine, Malika." Raven

flashed a fake smile. "Your father asked Mr. Richardson to take you someplace safe."

"I know. You are coming, Raven?"

Raven's shoulders slumped. "No. I can't come with you, Malika, but you'll be safe with Mr. Richardson."

A tremble rolled through Malika's small frame and she choked on a sob. "Please, Raven."

"I'm sorry. I—I just can't." Raven clamped her bottom lip between her teeth.

Buzz's pulse leaped. Was that a quivering lip she was biting? Nah, this was Raven Pierre, career girl extraordinaire.

"Say goodbye to Raven, darlin'. Let's get you buckled in nice and tight." Buzz turned to duck into the hatch of the Jetstream.

Clawing at his arms, Malika wailed. "I want Raven."

She wasn't the only one.

Raven grabbed the handrails and leaned forward. "You'll be fine, Malika."

"No, no." Malika buried her face against Buzz's chest, and he patted her back.

Without Raven, his plan looked as though it was going to deteriorate rapidly. He liked kids, but this motherless little girl wasn't going to be too happy with his male companionship.

Raven sighed and launched forward, nearly

barreling into his back. "All right. I'll come along, at least to get you settled."

Malika sniffled and a big smile claimed half her face.

Buzz narrowed his eyes as he transferred Malika to Raven's waiting arms. The girl's cries had done more to convince Raven to come along than Buzz's assertions to her importance to President Okeke. Had he just fallen into a rabbit hole?

He sat at the controls while Raven buckled Malika into one of several seats facing the cockpit and retrieved two blankets from a bin on the side of the plane. She tucked the blanket around Malika, twitched the girl's pigtails and then buckled into the seat next to her.

She let out a breath. "Where to, flyboy?"

"Just relax and enjoy the ride." Buzz adjusted his headphones and flipped a few switches. No need to tell Raven their final destination. She'd just gotten used to the idea of traveling along with Malika. He didn't want her to go ballistic about the location just when she'd accepted her fate.

Buzz gave a final wave to the ground crew and Naru waiting next to the car, and then taxied down the abbreviated runway. The meeting at the hotel had probably ended by now, and everyone would know he'd taken off with the president's daughter.

He scanned the darkening skies and settled

back into his seat as he pulled on the throttle, sending the nose of his plane toward the heavens. He hadn't filed a flight plan with air traffic control, since he didn't want anyone picking up his trail.

The CIA wouldn't come after him, at least not yet. The Agency wouldn't want to anger President Okeke and if the president trusted his daughter's safety to him and Raven, the CIA would just have to deal with it…for now.

The plane climbed to cruising altitude and Buzz stretched his legs. He could use a cup of coffee about now. Too bad he wasn't flying one of the big commercial jets. He glanced over his shoulder at Raven flipping through a magazine she must've had stashed in that huge bag of hers.

He preferred the company on this small plane to a bunch of overworked flight attendants anyway…even without the coffee.

Raven peeked over the top of her magazine. "Are we in for a long flight?"

"About seven hours." He pointed to Malika curled up in her seat, the blanket tucked up to her chin. "You should follow Malika's example and take a nap."

"Seven hours?" She dropped the magazine to her lap. "I guess I can't just land and turn around then."

"I didn't know that's what you'd planned. You volunteered to get Malika settled, remember?"

"Settled where, Buzz? Where are you taking us?"

He took a deep breath and shifted his gaze back to his control panel of blinking lights. "Oklahoma."

Raven gasped and then laughed, but the sound held no humor. Buzz had noticed that about Raven before. She could laugh but it didn't mean she was happy. That kind of laughter always made him uncomfortable, and it hadn't changed.

He twisted in his seat to find Raven's head touching her knees and her shoulders shaking from the laugh that wasn't a laugh. Buzz raised one eyebrow. "Why are you laughing?"

Not that he minded. He preferred it to her throwing things at him, especially when he was trying to fly.

Raven jerked her head up. "Come on, Buzz. Don't play the slow cowboy with me. You know why Oklahoma is significant."

"Because it was my home. Because I wanted to take you there after we married. Because it's where I wanted to raise a family...with you. But now it's just a safe place for Malika until Burumanda's political situation cools down and she can be reunited with her father." He shrugged. "Not significant at all."

"It *was* your home?" Raven brushed strands of her hair from her face. "You didn't return to Oklahoma after leaving Prospero?"

"No. I live in Dallas now, but I still have my folks' ranch in Oklahoma. I figure I can protect Malika there." He patted the empty co-pilot's seat next to him. "Do you want to join me up front? You were getting good at flying before…"

Before she'd taken off like a scared rabbit once he mentioned marriage, family and forever. Raven had never had an example of any of those things in her life. Her wealthy family had lived abroad, dropped Raven off at boarding schools and stashed her with nannies.

Obviously not wanting a trip down memory lane, Raven scrambled from her seat and lurched toward the cockpit. "Just tell me what to do."

"Nothing. Relax and enjoy the view."

After fifteen minutes of companionable silence as the Jetstream cut through the night sky, Raven tapped his shoulder. "Why didn't you settle in Oklahoma? It's all you ever talked about."

It's all he'd ever talked about? No wonder he'd scared her off.

He lifted the shoulder where her hand still rested. "Wasn't ready."

Once he retired from Prospero, he'd discovered all his plans for the ranch had become meaningless without Raven. And all the women he'd met since lacked Raven's spunk, her beauty, her sexiness, her...

She squeezed his shoulder. "Well, you'll get there one day. I know the ranch meant a lot to you after your parents died."

The transponder beeped and Buzz flicked his radar screen. "There's another private plane in the area. We're too low for a commercial airliner."

Raven slouched to peer out her side window. "Is it close enough that we'd see it? It's clear out here."

"It's behind us. You might be able to see its lights if you went to the back of the plane, but it's okay. He's not going to run into us or anything. We both have transponders."

Buzz tried to contact the other plane on the radio, but the pilot didn't respond. A muscle ticked in his jaw, and he clenched his hand on the steering wheel.

Raven's gaze took in his white knuckles and the straight line of his mouth. "Are you sure it's okay? Could that be the CIA after us?"

He shook his head. If it were the CIA, the pilot would be all over that radio giving him orders. If it were...someone else, the pilot might want to follow him silently.

"Buzz, you never told me what a commercial airline pilot was doing at the U.N. during President Okeke's address. And how did you get so chummy with the president that he'd let you fly off with his daughter?"

Buzz blew out a breath. He might as well tell her the rest. "Jack Coburn is missing."

"Jack?" Raven gripped the arms of her chair. "What happened?"

"We're not sure. He took a job as a hostage negotiator after Prospero. He disappeared in Afghanistan while on a job trying to negotiate the release of some doctor."

"What does President Okeke have to do with Jack's disappearance and why are you involved?"

"It's Jack."

She hugged herself, hunching her shoulders. "I know you guys would do anything for each other, but how is his disappearance related to President Okeke?"

Buzz rubbed his eyes. "It started with a drug deal between a Mexican cartel and a group of terrorists out of Afghanistan. Jack's name came up in the chatter. Riley was able to link the terrorists with an arms dealer."

"Riley Hammond, the Navy SEAL from Prospero? I thought he was taking tourists out on a dive boat in Cabo?"

"He took a detour to help out. We all did. Ian Dempsey located the weapon the terrorists bought with their drug money—turned out to be a biological weapon."

Raven covered her mouth with her hands. She'd worked with them at Prospero for a time, so Buzz felt sure not much shocked her. She'd been tough…and brittle since the moment he'd met her. The brittleness—that's what had sabotaged their relationship.

"If Ian had something to do with locating that weapon, it must've been in the mountains. Did he leave his job leading mountain-climbing expeditions?"

Buzz cocked his head. She sure knew a lot about his former comrades. "We all dropped everything as soon as we got the call from Colonel Scripps."

"I'm sure you did. And what's this third link? What does the biological weapon Ian recovered have to do with President Okeke?" Her eyes widened. "You don't think he's in the market for this biological weapon, do you?"

"I wasn't sure—" he glanced back at the slumbering Malika "—because it was rumored he had ties to some terrorist groups, but after I met with him I think he's clean. The Agency also believes Okeke has the means to deliver a virus, weaponize it."

Raven hugged herself. "That's scary."

"That might be what the rebels are after, or maybe someone is using the rebels to get to Okeke. The region of Burumanda, before it was a country, was a hotbed of terrorist training activity. A lot of terrorist groups around the world wanted to keep it that way."

Pressing her fingers against her temples, Raven closed her eyes. "Why isn't anyone else looking for Jack? Why is it up to you guys? None of you is even on active duty anymore."

Buzz ground his teeth together. This was the hardest part. "The CIA thinks Jack turned. They think he leaked information to the terrorists, is maybe feeding them intelligence about the delivery method for this virus."

Raven's eyelids flew open. "No way. That's not possible."

"That's exactly why I'm here."

"I-is the CIA, I mean, are they going to suspect you kidnapped Malika to get information about Jack?"

"*Kidnapped* isn't the right word." He scratched his chin and yawned. "I took her with her father's permission, but I'm sure they'll suspect I did it for my own reasons."

"And did you? You're not using that little girl, are you?"

Buzz shook his head at Raven's sharp tone. She'd become very protective of Malika in a short space of time. Must be because she'd saved her life, or at least saved her from a kidnapping. "You know me better than that, Raven. I'm the kid-friendly one around here. If I didn't think I could do a better job of keeping Malika safe than a bunch of by-the-book spooks at the Agency, I wouldn't have taken her."

"You're right." She sighed and pushed her hair back from her face. "I'm still on edge…and I missed my date."

"Aww, I'm sorry. Let me guess. Broadway show and a hip new restaurant? Or a tapas bar and some club in the Meat Packing District?"

"It all sounds so shallow when you put it like that, Buzz." She unbuckled her seatbelt and slid from her co-pilot's perch. "But a helluva lot more fun than sitting on a porch sipping lemonade and watching horses run around. Now I'm going to try to get some sleep before we arrive in Nowheresville, Oklahoma."

Six hours later and with no other planes invading his air space, Buzz landed his Jetstream safely at the small White Cloud municipal airport. The morning sun streaked across the broad expanse of sky like a runny egg yolk. His stomach rumbled and he figured their first stop would be breakfast at the Arapaho Café.

He taxied to a stop next to the hangar and completed his post-flight check. Rubbing his eyes, he turned in his seat to face his sleeping passengers. Raven had reclined both seats, and her long legs were stretched out in front of her while Malika was curled into a tight ball, her head resting on Raven's shoulder. At least she wasn't drooling this time.

He should get a picture for blackmail purposes.

Hunching forward, he entered the cabin and nudged Raven. "We're here."

Raven started and grasped the arms of her seat, digging her long nails into the leather. "What? Already?"

"We've been flying for six hours. It's morning, or almost."

Raven stretched out a hand and touched Malika's cheek. "Malika? Time to wake up."

Buzz squinted out the window, running his tongue across his teeth. If only he'd had time to pack a bag with a toothbrush. And if he felt that way, Raven must be itching for a shower and some clean clothes. Of course she wouldn't be able to buy any designer duds in White Cloud, and they needed to get that little girl something to eat first.

Malika opened her big brown eyes with a flash of fear, until her gaze settled on Raven and the anxiety melted away.

"Are you hungry?" Raven tweaked one of Malika's pigtails. "Buzz, we're going to need something to eat before anything else."

Buzz raised his brows. Who had stolen his tough-as-nails Raven and left this squishy marshmallow in her place? "Sure. I was thinking the same thing. After I check in with the ground crew, we'll hitch a ride into town. I doubt there's anything to eat at the ranch."

They disembarked, and Buzz bundled Raven and Malika inside the hangar while he secured the plane. One of the guys at the airport agreed to loan Buzz his truck.

As Buzz squeezed Malika between himself and Raven in the front seat of the truck, Raven's jaw dropped. "You mean this guy who's a stranger is letting you take off in his truck? How does he know we're not going to hit the highway and steal it?"

Buzz chuckled as he threw the beat-up truck in Reverse. "He has my Jetstream. I'd say that's a fair trade."

"How does he know you didn't steal that plane?"

"It's called trust. There's a lot of that in a small town. Besides, there are no strangers in White Cloud. That guy is cousins with my best friend's ex-girlfriend."

Raven rolled her eyes. "If you say so."

They bumped along in the truck for a few miles before they careened into town. The streets were mostly empty at this time of morning, except for a couple of trucks parked in front of the Arapaho

Café. Retired ranchers up at their customary time and looking for a little company.

And Buzz probably knew all of them.

Scratching his chin, he shot a glance at Raven and Malika. He couldn't exactly tell the good people of White Cloud that he was hiding an African president's daughter in their midst. The assassination attempt at the U.N. had been splashed all over the news, but Malika's picture hadn't been splashed anywhere. The government had suppressed any news of her attempted abduction and Raven's role in her rescue.

He blew out a breath and squared his shoulders. The plan came to him in a flash and Raven might even laugh about it...someday.

He pulled up to the curb and pointed to the restaurant. "I hope you ladies are hungry."

Buzz yanked his coat around his wrinkled suit and opened the door of the truck for Raven. She hopped out and scooped Malika from the seat. "Ahh, I can smell the bacon from here."

"Bacon, eggs, biscuits and gravy. The Arapaho has it all." Buzz pushed open the door and several pairs of eyes turned in their direction.

"Well, if it isn't Buzz Richardson."

"Must've dropped out of the sky."

"It's Steve's boy."

Raven stiffened beside him as he raised his

hand in greeting. "Hey, guys. It's good to be back."

"Whatcha doing here, Buzz? You gonna take up residence at the ranch?"

Buzz shrugged out of his coat and hung it on the rack by the front door. "Just thought it was time to bring my wife and our new daughter home to White Cloud."

Chapter Four

Raven squeezed Malika's hand so tightly the girl whimpered. She immediately loosened her hold, but still had a death grip on the back of the chair with her other hand. If she squeezed any harder she'd snap the wood.

Raven's stiff face formed a wooden smile as she met the curious gazes of the old men seated around a red Formica table. She peeled her fingers from the chair and waved like a queen from her motorcade.

She'd kill Buzz.

Buzz winked at her and grabbed her hand, pulling her toward the group. He performed a round of introductions, but the names whirred through her brain, replaced by the surprise at the warmth of their greeting. After each introduction, the men jumped to their feet and pulled her in for a kiss on the cheek, their gray whiskers tickling her chin.

Then they turned their attentions to Malika.

They tugged lightly on her pigtails and chucked her beneath the chin. She seemed to take it much more in stride than Raven. At the end of the introductions, the old guys had Malika grinning and giggling as though she'd just discovered a roomful of doting grandfathers.

Buzz held up his hands. "That's enough socializing. My girls are tired and hungry."

The men grumbled but went back to talking about…whatever old men talk about in a diner in the wee morning hours.

Raven glared at Buzz as he pulled out her chair. She even flared her nostrils for added effect. He grinned at her and lifted Malika into her seat.

After the waitress took their order, Raven folded her hands on top of the plastic menu. "Why did you tell them we were married?"

"It was the best cover I could think of on short notice." He slid a blue crayon toward Malika, who had her head bent over a children's menu, ready for coloring. "Until I saw that bunch sitting at the table, it didn't occur to me how suspicious I'd look marching into town with a woman and a little girl from Africa at my side."

Raven snapped her brows over her nose. "I thought it was your job to think of things like that. You had an entire seven-hour plane ride to think of a story."

"It's a good story, Raven." He shrugged.

"Nobody in White Cloud needs to know we're hiding some African president's daughter. The world at large doesn't even know she's missing. Most people in diplomatic circles don't even know President Okeke brought her."

"Have you had contact with the president?"

"On his orders, no. He doesn't want her location to be compromised at all. We're supposed so stay here with her until further notice."

Malika glanced up from her coloring through dark lashes. "My father does not want me to talk of him."

Buzz patted her hand. "We know that, Malika. You're a smart girl."

Raven's nose tingled. How easily this little girl adapted to subterfuge. She shouldn't have to live her young life like that.

"Do you understand our game, Malika?" Raven tucked a stray curl behind Malika's ear. "While we're here in White Cloud, we're going to pretend we're a family. Just until we can get you safely back to your father."

Malika lodged the tip of her tongue in the corner of her mouth while she colored in a tiny bird. Then she looked up. "I understand...Mama."

The tingling in Raven's nose spread to her eyes, which flooded with tears. She scrabbled for a napkin from the dispenser on the table and pressed it to her eyelids. Then she blew her nose.

Avoiding Buzz's gaze, Raven rapped her knuckles on the table in front of Malika. "Our food's going to be here in a minute. Let's wash our hands."

Malika dropped her crayons and hopped from her chair. Raven crossed the small dining room to the restroom, her high heels clicking on the floor. If they were going to stay here for a while, and it looked as if they were, she'd have to buy some clothes for her and Malika. High heels and silk suits wouldn't cut it in this little backwater town.

They finished washing up and pushed out of the ladies' room. As they passed the old men, one called out. "So where'd you meet Buzz, Raven?"

"Umm, at work." Might as well keep this as close to the truth as possible.

"What are you, a stewardess?"

"Ah, I meant at his previous job."

The man's shaggy gray brows shot up. "You were in the military?"

Oh boy. Nothing was going to be simple. Of course, Buzz could never be open and honest about what he did. He was in covert ops. He was a spy. He'd lived his life in the shadows with secrets that could topple governments.

And she'd helped him. She'd been a member of Prospero. Translating, teaching, training.

Falling in love.

"Oh, on the civilian end. I'm a translator." She waved her hands as if to brush off his question and stumbled back to the table toward the heavenly scent of bacon.

Buzz waved a knife at the old ranchers. "Giving you the third-degree back there?"

Raven spread a napkin on her lap and pointed to Malika's lap. "Asked where we met. I said we met at work, where I was in a civilian capacity."

"That'll do." He slid a basket of biscuits toward her. "Biscuits and gravy?"

She gave a slight shudder and plucked a biscuit from the basket. "No on the gravy, but I might try one with honey."

She pulled the biscuit in half and drizzled a little honey on one side. She bit into the biscuit and closed her eyes as it melted into her mouth. "I may have to shop for one size up if I stay here and keep eating like this."

Buzz held his fork suspended over his plate. "That means you're staying?"

"You pretty much sealed my fate back there." She jerked her thumb over her shoulder at the table of gossiping men.

"You could always find an excuse to leave, Raven." He dropped his fork and handed a napkin to Malika. "You did before."

Heat flashed across Raven's cheeks. He was the one who'd changed the rules. She slid a glance toward Malika, who was clutching her fork between coiled fingers. Could she sense the tension at the table? Hadn't Raven always been able to sense the tension in her family?

"Nope." Raven brushed the biscuit flour from her fingertips. "No excuses. We're in this together. This is our make-believe, right, Malika?"

Malika smiled, nodded and shoveled some scrambled eggs into her mouth.

When they finished their breakfast, they said goodbye to the men still nursing their coffee in the corner. As Buzz swung open the door, a short, stocky man barreled through it, almost colliding with Buzz.

"Sorry…" The man trailed off and his eyes narrowed beneath his cowboy hat. "Buzz Richardson, hotshot pilot."

His sharp tone cut across the café and Raven took a step back. Guess not everyone in White Cloud was friendly.

"Lance, how have you been?" Buzz stuck out his hand but the smaller man ignored it.

"Could be better, Buzz. Could be better." He turned on his heel and stalked to an empty table.

With his jaw tight, Buzz ushered Raven through the door. They stepped into the chilly Oklahoma morning, and Raven pulled her coat around her body.

"What was that all about? I thought everyone in White Cloud was your best friend."

"That's Lance Cooper."

"So?" She circled one finger in the air. "I'm supposed to know him?"

"He's the brother of Josh Cooper, the man who was flying my parents in my plane when it crashed."

Raven gasped. "Buzz..."

He shook his head and opened the passenger door of the truck. She understood that signal.

Raven cleared her throat. "When do the stores open? We're going to have to get some basics and Malika and I need some clothes."

His shoulders relaxed. "It's Saturday. The stores open around nine. We'll head out to the ranch first and make the place livable for the next few weeks."

"Few weeks?" Raven buckled Malika into the seat between them. "Is that how long you think this is going to take?"

Buzz cranked on the engine of the old truck. "I'm not sure, Raven. We'll see how things work out."

In less than five minutes, they hit open road. Raven gazed across the flat landscape with a few low hills in the distance. The sky was wide open and looked as if it could gulp up everything in its sphere. The rising sun gleamed on the dusky browns and golds and then shimmered across an expanse of aqua blue, the color of Buzz's eyes.

She tapped her window. "What's that?"

"That's Lake Unega. There's a lot of activity around the lake during the summer—fishing, waterskiing, boating. Luckily this isn't summer."

Raven shivered and tucked her arm around Malika. "No kidding. It's not going to snow while we're here, is it?"

"We don't usually get much snow, maybe a light dusting." He tweaked the folds of her cashmere coat. "That old rag should do you just fine."

"Don't pull that down-home crap with me, Richardson. You're the best-dressed cowboy I've ever seen." His gloom after running into Lance Cooper seemed to have lifted, and she was happy to give it the heave-ho. This sadness was a new side of Buzz she'd never seen before.

"See many cowboys in New York City, do you?"

Malika bounced on the seat between them, enjoying the lighter mood. "Where is your hat? Where is your hat?"

Buzz laughed and the sound warmed up the car. "I have one at home, and I'm going to get you one, too. Would you like that?"

"Yes, and those, please." Malika pointed to Raven's high heels planted on the plastic mat of the truck.

"You'll have plenty of time for those." Grinning, Buzz met Raven's eyes over the top of Malika's head.

His smile encased her in warmth and she suddenly felt as if she had been locked in a deep freeze for a long time. Two years and eight months, to be exact. Since the day she'd left him.

Her bottom lip trembled, and she turned and pressed her forehead against the cold glass of the window. She hadn't even been there for him when he'd lost his parents. "Almost there?"

"Willow Road Ranch is just around the next bend."

"It has a name and everything?"

"Thought I told you all about it."

His clipped words made her bite her lip. He'd told her all about the ranch where he'd grown up. The more he'd talked about it, the more evident it had become that he planned to stash her there after their marriage. So the more she'd tuned him out.

"Did you tell me why it was called Willow Road Ranch?"

"Wait and see."

He wheeled the truck around the bend and turned down a paved road. One more turn and the asphalt gave way to something less civilized. The tires of the truck crunched and spewed gravel in a cloud of dust and then trundled between the reaching branches of a line of willow trees. The thin sticks, bereft of leaves, created a spiky tunnel toward the sprawling ranch house that lay ahead.

Raven pressed her nose to the window. "This must be beautiful in the spring when the trees have all their leaves."

"It is." He nudged Malika's rounded shoulder. "Looks like she needs a nap before you go on your shopping spree."

Sighing, Raven blew a puff of air against the glass. This hideaway was going to be a minefield of emotions for both of them. Buzz had wanted to have their wedding right here on the ranch… in the spring.

Buzz had invited her to White Cloud several times to meet his parents and his sister, but she'd always found some excuse. Now she'd never meet his parents.

The truck rolled to a stop around the circular drive, and Buzz tipped his chin toward a garage at the end of the property. "My truck should be in there, and then I can return this one to its rightful owner."

"I still can't believe he just let you take his truck."

"That's White Cloud."

Raven left the door of the truck open as she

leaned against the hood. "The house looks pretty good for being abandoned."

"It's not exactly abandoned." Buzz ducked into the truck and scooped up a sleeping Malika. "My manager, Shep Ochoa, has been with our family for years. He takes care of the ranch, and one of his daughters makes sure the inside is habitable. So we should have clean sheets, warm water and a working furnace and electricity."

Raven stretched. "Sounds like heaven about now. Keys?"

"Under the mat, of course."

"I'll unlock the door while you keep a tight hold on our precious cargo."

Buzz adjusted Malika's drowsy form so that her head rested on his shoulder.

Gulping, Raven crouched down and swept her hand beneath the mat. The man was a natural. The fact that some woman hadn't snapped him up yet surprised the heck out of her. Surprised her and pleased her.

She jingled the keychain. "Probably right where you left them. Heckuva place, White Cloud."

Opening the door, she stepped aside to allow Buzz through with Malika. As he crossed the expansive great room to a door just beyond the staircase, Raven dropped the keys on a table and took a turn around the room.

Raven didn't know quite what she expected

from ranch décor, but she knew it wasn't this rustic room filled with charm and comfort. Sliding glass doors led to a wooden deck that commanded a view of the ranch, rolling hills fringing the landscape. A huge stone fireplace took up half a wall while Native American wall hangings graced another.

She dropped into a deep, rust-colored chair and kicked off her shoes just as Buzz appeared.

"Is Malika still sleeping?"

"Yeah, she mumbled a few words I didn't understand and then went out like a light. Guess she didn't sleep too comfortably on the plane." He perched on the edge of the sofa across from her and clasped his hands between his knees.

"Probably had a lot to do with all the excitement and terror of running through the U.N. with me."

"I'm impressed at how you handled yourself, Raven. Those years in Prospero must've rubbed off on you."

A lot had rubbed off on her. Hunching her shoulders, she folded her arms. "That little girl is resilient and she shouldn't have to be. It's not fair."

"It's good to be resilient. Look at you."

Raven snorted. She'd hardly hold herself up as an example to anyone. Didn't Buzz realize her resiliency was what kept her from making a commitment to marriage and family?

"Yeah, just look at me." She spread her arms and stretched her legs in front of her.

"You don't even have a toothbrush, and you're not falling apart."

"Don't remind me or a total breakdown just might be around the corner."

Buzz pushed up from the sofa and yawned. "I think I'm going to follow Malika's lead and get some sleep. I have some toothbrushes in one of the bathrooms if you want to freshen up a bit before hitting the shops."

"Maybe I'll do that." She snagged her purse from the floor. "You know, I haven't even checked my messages since we literally flew out of New York. Maybe my boss, Walter, has some news."

"Just don't tell him where you are. Don't tell anyone."

"Got it." Raven slid open her phone and frowned—a text message from a restricted number. "This could be Walter."

She clicked the button to open the message and gasped. She dropped the phone. It hit the coffee table and bounced to the hardwood floor.

Buzz jerked his head up. "Bad news?"

Raven licked her lips. "I just got a message from Malika's would-be kidnappers. And they're not happy with me."

Chapter Five

Adrenaline pumped through Buzz's body and he clenched his hands, ready to do battle with unseen enemies. He dropped to the floor to retrieve Raven's phone and flipped it open. Reading the message, his jaw tightened.

Return the girl or die.

As Raven said, the message came from a restricted number, but that didn't mean they couldn't trace it back to a cell phone. But how did these maniacs get Raven's phone number? And how did they know she had Malika?

Raven rubbed her palms on her slacks. "It's just a message, right? They don't know where we are."

"How do they know you have her?" Buzz tapped the phone against his palm. "And how did they get your number?"

Hunching her shoulders, Raven shoved her nervous hands into her pockets. "They knew she was in that anteroom at the U.N. and probably knew she was with a female translator. There are several ways they could've gotten my name. Same goes for my cell phone number. Maybe they're just guessing she's with me."

"Would your office give out your number?"

"Under the right circumstances. Look, these guys were able to infiltrate the General Assembly with weapons. They probably have someone on the inside."

"You're good, Raven Pierre." He held up the phone. "I'm going to see if we can get a trace on this restricted number."

"Be my guest." She pulled her hands out of her pockets and hugged herself, which should've been his job. "The message is meaningless, just an empty threat…right?"

"You and Malika are safe here, Raven. If any strangers show up in White Cloud, I'll check them out."

She relaxed her shoulders and attempted a smile. "Yeah, those old coots at the Arapaho would have a line on any stranger in under ten minutes."

"That's right." He brushed a strand of black hair from her cheek. "Just don't let them hear you calling them *coots,* especially old ones."

"Are you still tired? You're the one who flew all night."

"You go ahead and take a nap. I'll check out

the phone and then hit the sack. Then I'll take you and Malika into town for some shopping." He gestured at her sophisticated ensemble. "You'd better get yourself a pair of jeans and some boots…the kind without five-inch stiletto heels."

"I think I can manage that. Bed?"

Buzz raised one eyebrow. He could make a salacious joke right now, but the image of Raven sprawled across his bed upstairs had him tongue-tied. A slow flush crept up Raven's neck and settled in her cheeks.

"I—I mean is there a bed for me somewhere." She pressed her hands to her face. "A bedroom I can use?"

Clearing his throat, Buzz said, "There are plenty of bedrooms upstairs and a few should be made up. When you get to the top of the stairs, hang a left. The yellow room on the right should be good to go."

"Thanks." She snagged her bag and heaved it over her shoulder.

Buzz stopped her halfway to the staircase. "Clean towels and those toothbrushes I promised are in the cupboard in the hallway."

"Wake me up by noon, sooner if Malika wakes up."

He nodded and watched the sway of her hips as she ascended the stairs, high heels dangling from two fingers. Swallowing hard, he smacked the counter that ran between the great room and the country kitchen as he perched on a stool.

Did he think it was going to be easy having his ex-fiancée parading around his house? Sleeping in one of his beds? Just not *his?*

His subconscious must've jumped into action when he'd been thinking up a cover story for them on the fly. How convenient to pretend Raven was his wife. He'd always believed he could get her to change her mind about their relationship if she'd only spend some time in White Cloud.

Deep down Raven yearned for the very things she pushed away with both hands. Home. Family. Stability. She'd never had them, so she pretended she didn't want them, figured they were out of her reach. But he knew better.

Buzz smacked the counter again. Get over it, man. How'd that saying go? *She's just not that into you.*

He pulled his own cell phone from his pocket, one of many untraceable models he carried. He punched in the number for Colonel Scripps, one of the men behind Prospero, and the man who had assembled the former Prospero team members to find Jack Coburn.

"Colonel, it's Buzz."

"You've stirred up a hornet's nest at the Agency and with those guys from the Dignitary Protection Division. Seems you took off with President Okeke's daughter, and they're none too pleased with the kidnapping."

"Kidnapping?"

"That's what they're calling it."

Buzz scraped his stool back and hunched over the counter. "I made previous arrangements with President Okeke. Did they tell you that?"

"President Okeke is keeping mum."

Buzz worked his jaw. "He's not accusing me of kidnapping his daughter, is he?"

"No, but he hasn't mentioned any special arrangements either, which has the CIA hopping mad…at you."

"I have no intention of tipping off the Agency as to my whereabouts, Colonel. I'm keeping this little girl safe until the trouble in Burumanda settles down."

"And?"

"And what?"

"You're going to keep her safe until the unrest in Burumanda is over and until you find out what it all has to do with Jack?"

Buzz scratched his chin. "You accusing me of using a little girl as collateral for intel on Jack?"

The colonel coughed. "I know you wouldn't do anything to put that girl in harm's way, Buzz. But I also know you wouldn't relinquish an opportunity to gather information on Jack's situation."

"I do know the same terrorist group that sold drugs to finance a biological weapon is the same terrorist group that's behind the attempt on Okeke's life and the foiled kidnapping of his daughter. This group is linked to Jack's disappearance and our old nemesis, Farouk, is leading the charge."

"Speaking of the foiled kidnapping, I understand our own Raven Pierre saved the day."

His own Raven Pierre. Buzz traced a pattern on the tile countertop with his fingertip. "Yeah, Raven put her Prospero training to good use."

Colonel Scripps let out a long breath on the other end of the line. "Is she with you?"

Buzz choked. "Is Raven with me? You know better than that, Colonel."

"Sure, I know better."

"I called for a favor." Buzz twirled Raven's cell phone on the tile. "Can you get a trace on a restricted number sending a text to a cell phone?"

"I can use my sources to give it a try, but if it was a pre-paid phone sending the text, it can't be traced. If this person calls again, get me on another line and we can try to get the phone company to use the tower triangulation to locate the general location of the caller."

Fat chance of that happening. Buzz gave the colonel the information from Raven's cell phone anyway, avoiding any mention of Raven herself or the text of the message. Colonel Scripps had enough to worry about. He didn't need to think about one of his agents on a mission with Buzz's ex-fiancée.

Buzz ended the call and stretched, glancing at his watch. Maybe he would get a little shut-eye before he took Raven and Malika into town. He bolted the front door and looked in on Malika. That little girl had done a number on Raven. Or maybe Raven believed in that Chinese proverb that once she'd saved Malika's life, she was responsible for her forever.

He took the stairs two at a time and eased open the door to the yellow room. A lavender fragrance still wafted from the connected bathroom, but Raven was out cold in the bed.

Buzz crept into the room and tugged the covers over Raven's bare shoulders and up to her chin. He closed his eyes as desire, strong and potent, coursed through his blood stream.

If Farouk didn't kill him, being holed up with his beautiful, untouchable ex-fiancée would.

RAVEN'S EYELIDS FLEW OPEN and her heart pounded. A dream. It was just a dream. Someone had been pursuing her through the halls of the U.N. She'd been running and running but couldn't find Malika. Malika's screams were growing fainter and fainter.

Wiping a hand across her mouth, she rolled to her side. She held her breath. A scream—a real one this time—resounded from downstairs. She scrambled out of bed and stumbled toward the door, realizing she'd shed her clothing before crawling between the sweet-smelling sheets.

She snatched her blouse from the back of the chair and shoved her arms into the sleeves. Tripping down the stairs, she fumbled with the buttons with trembling fingers.

When she hit the bottom step, Buzz called from the landing. "What is it? What's going on?"

"It's Malika. She's screaming." Raven swung around the corner of the balustrade and rushed to the open bedroom door where the cries had subsided to whimpers.

She careened into the room and pounced on Malika's bed. "Shh, what's wrong, sweetie?"

Malika pressed her small body against the headboard, her eyes wide. "The men are coming. The men are coming to get me."

Raven pried Malika from the headboard and clamped the girl's waiflike frame to her chest. "It's okay, Malika. The men aren't here. You're safe. You're safe with me and Buzz."

Malika snuffled against Raven's shoulder and rolled her head to the side. "Mr. Buzz is here."

Raven cranked her head over her shoulder, her gaze sweeping down all six feet three inches of

Buzz standing in the doorway, clad in a pair of faded blue jeans hanging low on his slim hips.

"Is everything okay?"

Raven nodded. "I think Malika had a bad dream, and she's not the only one."

Buzz twisted his wrist to peer at his watch. "It's just about noon anyway. Time to go into town."

"Would you like that, Malika?" She stroked the girl's hair. "Do you want to buy some clothes and eat some lunch?"

"Yes. I had a dream." A tremble rolled through her body and Raven squeezed her tighter.

"I had a dream, too. I'll bet it was the same dream, but we're safe now. Do you want to take a bath before we go out?"

"Yes, and then we buy clothes?"

Spoken like a true fashionista. "That's right. You have your priorities straight. Is there a bathroom downstairs with a tub, Buzz?"

He pointed to the ceiling. "Upstairs."

Malika scooted out of bed and Raven held her hand as they followed Buzz up the staircase.

Raven opened the cupboard door and filched a toothbrush for Malika. "Go in my bathroom and brush your teeth. I'll start the bath."

Raven squeezed some toothpaste on Malika's toothbrush and cranked on the water in the tub.

She squirted a steady stream of pink liquid into the steaming water and tossed the bubble bath bottle back into the basket at the head of the tub. The ranch house was completely outfitted and ready for a family.

When Raven returned to the bedroom, Buzz was propping up the doorjamb with one bare shoulder. She steered clear of conducting an inventory of the rest of his body. She knew it well—slabs of hard muscle shifting across his chest, a six-pack of ridges so firm you could balance a glass of wine on them, biceps strong enough to keep you safe forever.

She scooped up her bra from the chair, along with her slacks and shivered beneath her light blouse. Apparently, Buzz wasn't bothering with the niceties like she was. His gaze raked her body and she shivered again, this time under the hot intensity of his stare.

Glancing down, she cursed under her breath. In her haste, she hadn't buttoned her blouse properly. One edge of the blouse revealed the curve of her hip as the buttons gaped across her chest, practically baring one breast. The pulse in her throat beat a slow, seductive rhythm.

Buzz took one step toward her and she gulped. Her skin tingled as if he already had his hands on her.

"I am finished, Raven." Malika's clear voice cut through the sultry air between Raven and Buzz.

Raven snapped back to reality and climbed into her wrinkled slacks. She adjusted the buttons on her blouse and tossed the bra onto the bed. "Be right there."

She helped Malika undress and steadied her as she climbed into the oversized tub. "Buzz, can you please get Malika a towel?"

"I'm on it."

Leaving the bathroom door open, Raven stepped back into the bedroom just as Buzz appeared in the doorway, clutching a yellow towel. He tossed it to her.

She clutched it to her chest, all too aware of her peaked nipples brushing against the fabric of her blouse. She ducked into the bathroom and put the towel on top of the closed toilet seat.

"Are you okay in here?"

"I can bathe by myself, Raven."

"Well, I'm sure you can, but I'm going to be right here in the next room if you need me." Since Raven's little brother had drowned, she'd always been leery of kids and water.

She scooted past Buzz and scooped her bra from the bed. "Did you get much sleep?"

"A little. You?"

She turned her back on Buzz and shrugged

out of her blouse. She shimmied into her bra and slipped back into her blouse, buttoning it correctly this time. No slices of bare skin. Tucking the blouse into her slacks, she turned to face him.

"I was sleeping just fine until I had that dream. Someone was chasing me through the U.N."

"Makes sense."

His blue eyes still smoldered, and Raven shifted a nervous glance down at her neckline.

"Don't worry. Everything's in place…but not before I got an eyeful."

Warmth suffused Raven's cheeks and she slipped her feet into her Jimmy Choos. Nothing like a little height to regain your composure. "Watch it, Buzz. You're sounding a little desperate."

"Maybe that's because I am a little desperate."

"I'm done, Raven. All clean."

Which was more than Raven could say for her thoughts.

"Okay. Grab your towel and let's go shopping."

Twenty minutes later as they headed out the front door, Buzz dangled a set of keys in front of Raven. "You take my truck and follow me back to the White Cloud Airport. I want to return our Good Samaritan's truck."

"Maybe he figured you were a goner and took off in your Jetstream." She snatched the keys from him. "Is your truck going to start?"

"That's one of Shep's jobs. Remember I told you about Shep Ochoa, our ranch manager? He's supposed to take the truck out for a spin now and then, so she should be good to go."

"Do you want to ride with me or with Buzz?" For some ridiculous reason, Raven held her breath. But not for long.

Malika jabbed a finger in her direction while Buzz quirked an eyebrow.

Raven grabbed the door handle and stopped. "Isn't she supposed to be riding in a car seat? What's the law in Oklahoma?"

"I have no idea, but I can ask the sheriff before we get a ticket."

Raven followed Buzz back down the highway and through the quaint town of White Cloud, now bustling with a noontime crowd. The Christmas season was approaching but they still had to get through Thanksgiving. Christmas in a small town would be interesting…different. Of course, it couldn't compare to Manhattan.

Not that she'd be spending her Christmas or even her Thanksgiving in White Cloud. Hopefully, she'd be out of here in a few days.

She waited for Buzz outside the small airport, just an airstrip really, while he shook hands and exchanged conversation with his new best friend. Buzz had flown into this town knowing he'd get to his ranch one way or another. Comforting.

He hopped into the truck beside her and winked at Malika in the backseat. "Are you girls ready to do some shopping at Daisy's?"

Raven's jaw dropped. "Daisy's? Really?"

Buzz smirked. "Don't worry. Daisy will have everything you'll need for a vacation in White Cloud."

"Just no pictures, please."

Buzz laughed and slapped the dashboard. He was enjoying this a little too much. He'd always played up their differences. He played the country hick from a small town and she embodied the cosmopolitan sophisticate educated at European boarding schools. But he was no hick and she felt like an impostor most of the time.

And when the hick and the sophisticate got together in bed…dynamite.

Raven pressed her knees together and sunk her teeth into her lower lip. She needed to sweep those thoughts from her mind. They had to take care of Malika, not get so involved in each other they forgot about her existence. Not like her parents did to her and her brother, Jace.

Squaring her shoulders against the seatback, Raven said, "Direct me to Daisy's."

"That's the adventurous spirit."

Raven cruised down the main street of town past the Arapaho, betting those old geezers were still stationed at their table gossiping. She pulled into a parking spot on the street.

Buzz shoved open his door. "Daisy's is on the corner. I'm going to stop in to see Sheriff Tallant and then take the truck over to the grocery store for some provisions."

She climbed out of the truck, dropped the keys in his palm and patted her purse. "Is there a bank or ATM nearby? I'd like to get some cash."

Buzz lifted the sexy cowboy hat he'd been sporting since they left the ranch and skimmed a hand through his short brown hair. "That's okay, Raven. Tell the salesclerk to put the clothes on my tab."

"Don't be ridiculous." She hoisted her heavy bag higher on her shoulder. "I can pay for my own clothes."

"No!"

Was this some kind of macho posturing? Raven placed her hands on her hips and opened her mouth. Then she noticed the grim set of Buzz's mouth and the muscle ticking in his jaw. The ATM. He didn't want her using the ATM or her credit card or anything else someone could use to trace her whereabouts.

The hands on her hips fisted, her nails digging crescents into her palms. Someone had sent her a text message, someone who believed she might have Malika. Someone knew her name.

She dropped her chin to her chest and aimed a glance at the top of Malika's head. "All right. They won't think I'm trying to pull one over on them, will they?"

"Nah. Just mention my name and the Willow Road Ranch."

"And I suppose I should drop that little bombshell about our marriage and adoption of Malika."

"That would help." He crammed the hat back on his head and dug into the pocket of his jacket for his wallet. He handed her a wad of cash. "This will help, too. If you spend more, because I know how much you like clothes, have them bill it to the ranch."

"You folks in White Cloud sure are a trusting bunch, and I'm pretty sure I'm not going to exceed my clothing budget here at Daisy's." She snatched the money from his hand and slipped it into her bag.

"You never know."

He tipped his hat and sauntered down the street in his tight jeans, looking every inch the cowboy. And she wanted to explore every inch of him... again.

Malika tugged on her hand. "Shopping."

Daisy's surprised Raven, and she picked up a couple of pairs of Levi's and some decent sweaters along with a pair of low-heeled boots. She also scooped up some underwear and a bra and while they weren't Victoria's Secret, they weren't granny panties either.

Her first pair of blue jeans thrilled Malika, and she insisted on a pair of rockin' red cowboy boots. The kid had taste.

As Raven heaped their purchases on the counter, the salesclerk smiled. "You must be new in town, or are you here for the rodeo?"

"Rodeo?" Raven tilted her head. "Um, no, we're sort of new, visiting. Uh, I'm Buzz Richardson's wife and this is our daughter."

Wow, that just rolled off her tongue.

The woman's eyes widened and then crinkled around the corners. "You don't say. Buzz is a favorite around here, even though he's been on the road for years. It's a shame about his folks. It's good that he's bringing family home."

The clerk continued to chatter while she rang up the clothes and didn't blink an eye when Raven admitted she didn't have enough cash to cover the total.

"I know Buzz is good for it, and if not—" she winked "—I know where to find him."

Raven gathered the bags, hanging some from her wrist and entrusting Malika with a few of the smaller ones. The salesclerk scurried to the door and held it open for them. Raven smiled her thanks.

"Buzz should be back with the truck any minute now."

"Shh." Malika put her finger to her lips and glanced both ways. "Buzz-Daddy."

"Oops. You're right. Buzz…Daddy." Raven had to admit it had a ring to it, just like that *wife* business.

Raven spotted Buzz's white truck at the only stoplight on the street, and she waved. When the light turned green, he made a U-turn and pulled up to the curb.

The door of the truck flew open and Buzz charged toward the sidewalk, clenching a piece of paper in his hand. He raised the crumpled paper in his fist. "This is not good."

Raven dropped the bags that were biting into her right hand. "What? What's wrong?"

He waved the sheet in front of her nose. "This. Not good."

She snatched the paper from his hand and read the brightly colored flyer announcing the White Cloud Harvest Festival and Rodeo. "What's the problem? The clerk in Daisy's mentioned something about a rodeo. Sounds fun…I mean, Malika would like it."

Buzz flipped off his hat and smacked it against his thigh. "Yeah, lots of fun, lots of strangers. We just lost our safe haven."

Chapter Six

Malika nestled in close to Raven's side, her small fingers curling around the bags in her hands. Raven met Buzz's eyes, creased at the corners with worry, and gave her head a slight shake. Malika didn't need any more turmoil or fear, and the girl had super-sensory radar for both.

Buzz plucked the flyer from Raven's hand and smoothed it out on the hood of his truck. "Sure, Malika would like it—cattle ropers, bull riders and rodeo clowns—what's not to like?"

"We finished our shopping." Raven held the bags up and swung them back and forth. "Now it's time for some lunch."

"There's a fast food place in town with a kids' play area. Will that work for everyone?"

Buzz's voice had a forced note of cheer, but Malika didn't notice. She'd already fixated on the words *fast food* and *play area*.

Raven clapped her hands. "Sounds great to me.

Nothing I like better than a processed burger, fries and screaming kids."

They stuffed the bags in the backseat of the truck where Buzz had already secured a booster seat. He lifted Malika into the truck and settled her in the seat. "You're not six years old yet, are you?"

Malika shook her head and held up five fingers.

"You're kidding me." Raven clapped a hand over her heart. "You're only five?"

Malika wiggled her five fingers, and Raven murmured to Buzz, "I thought she was about eight."

"Because you're such an expert on kids?"

Raven opened her mouth, thought better of it, and snapped it shut. Buzz still harbored a lot of resentment against her for ending their engagement. She'd let him wallow in it…for a while.

They pulled into the parking lot of the fast food restaurant and Raven shuddered. One of her worst nightmares, but they needed to keep Malika occupied while they discussed this latest wrinkle in their hideaway location.

They ordered some burgers and fries, which Malika wolfed down in under ten minutes. Then they ventured into the play area where Raven and Buzz hunched across a plastic table to hear each other after Malika had scampered toward the play structure teeming with screaming kids.

Buzz flattened the rodeo flyer on the table. "I had forgotten all about this. It couldn't come at a worse time."

"How big are we talking? I mean this is still White Cloud, Oklahoma, not Times Square on New Year's Eve."

"It's the biggest event we have." Buzz slumped in his chair, stretching his long legs in front of him. "We get a lot of strangers during the summer months, too, but the Harvest Festival is a big deal in this part of the state."

"You don't know every person in White Cloud as it is, Buzz. A bunch of strangers wandering around is not going to make that much difference. We can still keep Malika safe here, even with the rodeo in town."

"I hope you're right. People are going to start heading into town soon. Maybe it's already started." He gestured around the playroom at the screeching kids barreling down slides and chucking balls at each other in the ball pool. "It's crowded in here, even for a Saturday."

Raven waved at Malika, swinging from a rope. "We'll keep an eye on her. We'll protect her."

Buzz stared out the window. "You know, I used to think I could protect anyone."

Raven's heart lurched in her chest as she

covered Buzz's clenched hand with hers. She should've been with him when he lost his parents, but nobody had bothered to call her. The guys from Prospero must've thought she'd cause him even more pain. And maybe she would have.

"I still think you can protect anyone, Buzz." She slurped some soda through her straw. "Do you know Malika has a name for you already?"

"Really? Like I don't already have enough nicknames?"

"She calls you Buzz-Daddy. Sort of sounds like a fifties doo-wop group or something."

Buzz grinned. "And what does she call you?"

"Mama."

He dropped an over-salted French fry onto the waxy paper as his brows shot up. "Does it freak you out?"

"Funny enough, it doesn't." She shrugged and brushed her fingers together. "The kid's kinda growing on me."

"You saved her life."

"It's not like I had a choice. I saved my own, too." She planted her elbows on the table and rested her chin in her palms to cover her warm face. She really didn't know if she'd acted out of a desire to save Malika or her own hide. She'd leave the heroics to Buzz and his buddies. "So the rodeo's a big deal."

"The biggest in four counties. I'd forgotten all

about it. You know I haven't been back much
since my folks died."

She sucked in a breath. She hadn't known that.
The ranch had once been the center of his uni-
verse.

Carefully creasing a greasy napkin, she said,
"There are going to be strangers anywhere. Do
you really want to pick up and move Malika?"

"I can't move her at this point." Buzz shook
the ice in his cup. "My agreement with President
Okeke was to take Malika to White Cloud and
then have no further communication with him. I
can't contact him with a new location, and I can't
take off for parts unknown without his knowledge or approval. Then it really would be a kidnapping."

"Who's calling this a kidnapping?"

"The CIA. Colonel Scripps told me the Agency
is hopping mad that I absconded with the girl, but
the president and I figured the fewer people in on
the plan, the less likely we'd have to deal with a
betrayal."

Raven almost swallowed her fry whole. "You
suspect some betrayal from within the Agency?"

"We always suspect betrayal. You should know.
You were working that one mission when all four
members of Prospero were almost killed due to
sabotage."

"That was overseas where anything can happen on a mission. But here, Stateside? At the U.N.?"

"You said it, Raven. Anything can happen. Anywhere."

She crumpled the paper wrappings in her hand. She thought she'd had it made when she'd landed the job at the U.N. Safety. Security. Regular hours. No more chasing around after adrenaline junkies like Buzz and the rest of the Prospero gang. Had she missed the rush?

Not until Buzz had zoomed back into her life.

Raven looked up just in time to see Malika flying down the slide and land face-first on the AstroTurf.

Malika rubbed her cheek, but scrambled to her feet to take her chances again.

Buzz laughed. "I think we've had enough excitement for one day."

Raven put her hand on his arm. "Buzz, why haven't you been back to White Cloud? You loved this place."

The smile on his face dissolved. "That was before I lost my fiancée and killed my parents."

AFTER DINNER, BUZZ KNEADED the knot in his shoulder as he surveyed the kitchen. The place had a homier feel now, with food in the cupboards and the fridge and a child's laughter echoing from the family room. He hadn't been convinced that he could ever call the ranch home after the deaths of his parents and the estrangement from his sister. He still wasn't sure.

He folded his arms and wedged a hip against the kitchen counter. Maybe White Cloud hadn't been the smartest choice for Malika's hideaway. Maybe he hadn't been the smartest choice for her savior either.

After years of keeping other people's families safe, he'd failed when it had come to his own family.

Raven called from the other room. "Where's our water? Playing board games works up a mighty thirst."

"Mighty thirst. Soda." Malika's voice, stronger and surer than Buzz had ever heard it carried into the kitchen.

Raven poked her head around the corner, her face flushed and her eyes bright. She was actually enjoying playing games with Malika. She'd forged an incredible bond with the little girl.

"You can ignore that last request. Malika doesn't need any more soda." She slipped into the kitchen and hopped on top of the counter, her long legs dangling beneath her. "Is something wrong? Did you get some bad news from Colonel Scripps?"

"No." Buzz pushed off the counter and grabbed the handle of the fridge. "I was just thinking about the ranch. It feels like home today. After my folks died in that plane crash, it sucked the life out of this house."

Raven traced her finger along the grout of the tile. "You know, I didn't learn about the crash at the time it happened. I found out about a year later from Meg. None of the guys bothered to tell me. That's why I didn't call."

Ian Dempsey had been one of his comrades in Prospero and his wife, Meg, and Raven had hit it off the few times they'd met. Must've been their similar backgrounds—growing up with wealth and privilege, although Meg had shunned that lifestyle and Raven had embraced it.

Buzz had been so consumed with guilt at his parents' deaths at the time that he hadn't even noticed Raven's silence. She'd sent him a condolence card with a quick note almost a year after the crash. It had helped but made his return to the ranch even harder.

She wrapped her hand around his as he placed a glass of water on the counter. "Did the investigators ever find out what was wrong with the plane?"

"Poor maintenance."

"No way." She smacked the tile. "You took good care of that plane, Buzz. If anything, Josh should've checked the plane out more thoroughly before taking off."

"No." His hand jerked so violently, the water from the other glass sloshed over the sides. "It's not Josh's fault. I should've been there to fly that plane. It was my plane, my parents, my responsibility."

His gut twisted with the old pain, and he grabbed a dishcloth to mop up the water. He could forget when he was flying the commercial jets. He could forget in his apartment in Dallas. He could even forget while he was running around the globe looking for Jack Coburn. But the agony and guilt flooded his senses every time he stepped onto the ranch. Why did he think it would be any different this time?

Malika probably would've been safer in another location, where memories weren't constantly pummeling his brain and distracting him.

Raven slid the glass from the wet counter and turned toward the fridge. "I'll get another glass of water."

Buzz tossed the dishtowel into the sink and wiped his hand on the back of his jeans. Touching Raven's shoulder, he said, "Thanks for the card, by the way. I appreciated the gesture. I didn't know Meg had told you."

She spun around with a full glass of water in her hand. "Yeah, well, Meg knows what it's like to be shut out. Ian never told her anything about Prospero."

"They're back together now. He had to retrieve a case from the mountains in Colorado, where Meg's living and working. He found out they have a son together."

"Meg never told me she had a son."

"She never told Ian either. Once he got past his anger, he was thrilled." Buzz tried to keep the accusatory note out of his voice.

"I'm happy for them. I'm sure Ian will make a great dad." She turned away from him again, carrying the two glasses of water back into the family room.

He followed closely on her heels, a glutton for punishment. "Why are you so sure Ian will make a great dad after his upbringing with a couple of drunks, and yet you're so sure you'd be a failure?"

She put one glass down on the coffee table next to Malika and pressed her finger to her lips. Then she plopped on the floor and crossed her legs. "You didn't move my piece, did you, Malika?"

Clenching his jaw, Buzz perched on the end of the coffee table. Raven could dish it out, but she couldn't take it. She'd refused to examine her fears when she'd broken off their engagement and now, when proof that she could be a good parent was staring her right in the face with a pair of big brown eyes, she refused to acknowledge it.

Malika shoved a piece with her finger and shook her head. "Did not move."

"I was just teasing you, silly." Raven patted the top of Malika's head. "I think it's your turn."

Malika picked up a card and then dropped it on the board. "I would like to go to bed now."

"Are you feeling okay?" Raven put the back of her hand against Malika's forehead. "Do you want your water?"

"Yes, please." Malika gulped down the water and scrambled to her feet, encased in soft flannel pajamas.

With a furrowed brow, Raven followed Malika into the downstairs bathroom. Ten minutes later, she plodded into the family room with heavy footsteps. She sank onto the sofa and kicked her feet up on top of the coffee table.

"I guess I screwed that up."

Buzz rested his magazine on his chest. "What are you talking about?"

"Malika." Raven pointed to the closed door of Malika's bedroom. "She was having fun until I accused her of cheating. Maybe it's some kind of heavy insult in her culture. She didn't give me one smile before I tucked her in."

Buzz draped an arm across the back of the sofa, his fingers lightly touching Raven's shoulder. Her confidence in dealing with Malika must be shaky if it took so little to dash it.

"She's tired, Raven. We flew in last night,

shopping today and the play area. I'm exhausted, too."

"Yeah, she's tired of having a fraud for a parent. Any news on her father or Burumanda?"

"Nothing yet. I'll wait for the colonel to call me. Once the legitimate government takes control, they should both be safe in their own country."

Raven released a long breath and closed her eyes. Her long, dark lashes fluttered against her cheeks and Buzz brushed a wisp of hair from her throat. She parted her lips.

Touching no other part of Raven's body, Buzz covered her mouth with his. A pulse throbbed in her lower lip, and she curled one hand around the back of his neck. He deepened the kiss, stroking her cheek.

She tasted as good as he remembered and her skin, devoid of the expensive makeup she usually wore, felt soft and supple beneath his touch. Not that he minded the artfully applied makeup or the high heels or the designer clothes. Even in the field, Raven had dressed to kill—and he'd been her first victim.

As an adjunct member of Prospero, she'd been tough, brave, smart, witty and great in bed. A lethal mix.

She placed her hands flat against his chest, splaying her fingers across his T-shirt. "No strings?"

"No strings." He plowed his fingers through her black hair, the silky strands catching on the rough patches on his hands.

She plucked at his T-shirt and pulled it over his head. Goosebumps raced across his flesh as she trailed her long fingernails down his belly to the waistband of his jeans.

"Are you cold?" A smile played across her full lips.

"Baby, I'm burning up." He peeled her fleece sweatshirt from her shoulders, burying his face in her neck. Her fresh scent, enhanced by the Oklahoma countryside, intoxicated him to the point where it muddled the voice in his head yelling that this wasn't a good idea.

He gathered the material of her long-sleeved T-shirt in one hand and yanked.

"Hey, don't stretch this. It's brand-new." She smoothed the material before rolling it up and off her body.

The sexy, lacy bra cupping her perfect breasts couldn't have come from Daisy's. He unhooked it in the back and dangled it from his fingers. "I'm glad you didn't swap this out for the small-town version."

She reached for him, digging her nails into his shoulders. "Are you going to conduct an inventory of my clothes...or my body?"

Turning his head, he trailed a line of kisses along the inside of her arm. "I remember every inch of your body."

Raven shivered and grabbed his crotch. "And I remember every inch of you."

The laugh deep in his throat turned into a groan as the pressure of her hand increased. She unbuttoned his fly slowly and deliberately, each movement designed to heighten his desire.

Before she got to the last button, he straddled her and pinned her wrists against the cushions of the sofa. "Are you trying to tease me?"

She widened her eyes. "I'm just helping you undress. Would you like me to move a little faster?"

He dropped his head to her breast and circled her nipple with his tongue. "Mmm, I'm not that impatient. Are you?"

His hands shaped her breasts and she wriggled beneath him. "As a matter of fact, I..."

Her sentence trailed off along with his pleasure when a crash sounded from behind the closed door of Malika's room.

His mouth suddenly dry, Buzz jumped from the sofa and stepped over the coffee table, banging his knee. "That came from Malika's room."

Raven cried out and scrambled to follow him, repeating, "Oh my God. Oh my God."

Buzz shoved open the door and a gust of cold

air blasted him in the face. The window gaped open and a lamp lay shattered in pieces on the floor.

Malika was gone.

Chapter Seven

As Raven peered around Buzz's shoulder, her heart pounded from fear instead of passion. The words thumped against her temples with the same rhythm as her heart—*just like Mom and Dad, just like Mom and Dad.* She and Buzz had been too into each other to keep a close watch over Malika.

Buzz rushed to the open window and, grasping the windowsill, peered outside. "This window was locked. I know. I double-checked it earlier."

Clasping her trembling hands in front of her, Raven asked, "I-is the lock broken?"

Buzz stepped back and pulled down the window. With his brows a straight line across his nose, he inspected the glass and the lock. "I don't see any sign of forced entry."

Raven tiptoed around the broken glass from the lamp. "Could he have used some sort of tool to slip the lock?"

"I don't know, but we're not doing any good standing around talking about it." He charged from the room, buttoning his fly. He snagged his T-shirt from the back of the sofa, stuffed his feet into a pair of running shoes and threw open the closet door in the hallway by the front door.

"I'm coming with you." Raven had already pulled her shirt over her head and now reached past Buzz to grab her jacket. "They must've taken off on foot. We would've heard an engine."

Buzz raised one brow, his mouth a grim line. "A tornado could've ripped through the house and I don't think I would've heard it."

Leaning against the wall, Raven pulled on her new boots with shaking hands, her face hot. *Yep, just like Mom and Dad.*

"Just in case we can't find her on foot..." Buzz slipped his keys from a hook by the door and stepped onto the porch. "I'm going to investigate outside the window first."

Raven followed him around the corner of the house and could barely keep her balance on a pair of rubbery legs. Silent prayers tumbled through her brain. She narrowed her eyes against a gust of cold wind as they rounded the corner to the side of the house.

The windows of the house were low to the ground. The intruder hadn't needed any kind of boost to crawl into the room. Buzz crouched beneath the window and flicked his flashlight across the ground. "There are some broken flower stems and a few scuff marks against the side of the house."

A spurt of adrenaline rushed through Raven's system and she cried out. "Malika! Malika, where are you? I'll start in the back and you take the front."

"Oh no." Buzz clinched her around the waist. "I'm not leaving you on your own. We're doing this together."

Raven hadn't even thought about the danger to herself. Of course, Malika's abductor would be armed. And he wouldn't give up his precious cargo easily. The fate of a country rested on that little girl's shoulders.

Buzz clasped Raven's stiff, cold hand in his warm glove. At least someone had come prepared. He yanked her toward the front of the house and the circular drive, glancing down where his flashlight played across the ground.

"I don't see any new tire tracks. The footprints are harder to see."

They edged down the long drive, bordered by the bare willows. Their skinny branches created a lacy web that looked as if they could trap you. Raven snuggled closer to Buzz. The wind gusted again, lifting the ends of her hair and whipping it across her face.

"Malika? Malika?" Maybe if the girl was within hearing distance, she could give them a sign.

Cocking his head, Buzz shushed her. "Did you hear that?"

"What?" The only sound Raven could hear was the whistling wind that buffeted the ranch on all sides.

"The horses." Buzz jerked his thumb toward the barn to the left of the main house. "The horses are restless."

"Could it be the wind?"

"That or a stranger in their midst."

Raven rubbed her hands together. "Do you want me to continue toward the road while you check the horses?"

He placed a hand lightly on the back of her neck and steered her back toward the ranch. "I already told you, Raven. I'm not leaving you alone."

Glancing over her shoulder, Raven figured if the kidnapper had a car waiting outside the gates of the ranch Malika might be long gone. Her nose tingled and she rubbed it. Buzz could find her. Buzz could bring her back.

As they drew closer to the barn, the whinnying and snorting of the horses carried across the night. A knot formed in the pit of Raven's stomach. The knot tightened when she saw Buzz draw a gun from his pocket. He'd really come prepared.

They reached the barn door, and Buzz tucked her behind him. "Stay back."

He pushed open the door and flicked on the light. Raven blinked. She didn't even realize barns came equipped with electric lighting.

"Malika? Are you in here? Are you hiding?" Buzz lowered his weapon and peered around the corner of an empty stall.

"I wanted to see the horses."

At the small voice, relief coursed through Raven's body, so strong she sagged against the barn door.

Buzz disappeared into the stall. "You gave us a scare, young lady. I would've shown you the horses tomorrow."

He emerged from the stall, hoisting Malika in his arms, her pajama-clad legs and feet dangling over his hips.

An involuntary sob bubbled into Raven's throat and she coughed to stop it. Her fear turned to anger and she gritted her teeth to hold back the angry words balanced on the tip of her tongue. She closed her eyes and forced a smile to her stiff lips.

"You scared us, Malika. Why did you sneak outside? You don't even have a jacket."

Malika dropped her lashes and a violent tremble shook her small frame as if she'd just noticed the freezing temperature.

"I can solve that problem." Buzz opened his jacket and wrapped it around Malika. "Let's get you back to bed, and I promise I'll take you to visit the horses tomorrow. They'll be happier to see you then."

They trudged back to the house and Buzz carried Malika upstairs, bypassing the first-story bedroom. He nudged open the door of the room next to Raven's and pushed back the covers on the freshly made bed.

"I think you'll like this room better, but no climbing out of *this* window." He dropped a kiss on the top of Malika's head and left Raven to tuck her into bed.

Raven pulled the blankets up to Malika's chin. "Why did you climb out of that window?"

"The horses." Malika screwed up her eyes and wrinkled her nose.

Raven drew in a steady breath. She didn't want to vent her fear and anger on Malika, but she wouldn't be much of a parent if she let that flimsy excuse slide.

"Malika, I know the horses aren't the real reason why you climbed out of your window into the cold night wearing just your pajamas." Raven traced a finger around Malika's soft ear. "I won't get mad at you."

Malika opened one eye. "I heard you and Buzz-Daddy in the kitchen. You were mad. I am too much trouble."

"That's not true." Raven tugged Malika's ear

and smiled even though a little piece of her heart shattered.

"That is why my mother died. She had to stay with me instead of going with my father when the bad men came." A big, fat tear rolled down Malika's downy cheek.

Raven caught the tear with her thumb. "Your mother wanted to stay with you. And Buzz-Daddy and I want to stay with you, too."

Malika's wet lashes fluttered and she rubbed her nose against the pillow. "Horses."

Tucking the blankets around Malika's shoulders, Raven whispered, "That's right. You can visit the horses tomorrow. We can learn how to ride together."

Raven sat on the edge of the bed for several minutes more, watching the steady rise and fall of Malika's chest. She should've realized something had bothered Malika when she'd lost interest in their board game.

Nobody claimed parenting was easy. She'd just never had a desire to succeed at it…until now.

She left the bedroom door open when she stepped out of the room and tapped on Buzz's door.

"C'mon in."

Inching the door open, she peered around the edge. Her blood thudded through her veins as her gaze scanned Buzz's muscular frame propped up against snowy-white pillows. His touch had ignited a fire that burned like a pilot light in her belly. She knew now that flicker of heat between them would never die out.

He waved his book at her. "Come on in. I don't bite."

Liar. He did bite—intoxicating little nibbles that turned her insides to warm, sticky caramel. But she'd sworn off sweets.

"Malika climbed out that window because she heard us arguing in the kitchen. She thought we were arguing about her and she didn't want to be any more trouble to us."

"Silly kid."

The stress of losing Malika, the fear and anxiety of the past few days came crashing down on her like a detonated building. Sinking to her knees, she buried her face in her hands as sobs wracked her body.

Buzz's large, comforting hands clasped her shoulders. He drew her into his embrace, and her tears dampened his bare chest as she clung to him.

His lips caressed her temple. "Maybe you should go home. Maybe it was a mistake to drag you along."

Her head shot up and she ran a hand beneath her nose. "You don't think I can handle this? You don't think I can take care of Malika?"

"That's not what I meant." He tucked her hair behind her ears and cupped her face. "It's dangerous and stressful. I had no right to upend your life."

"It wasn't you, Buzz. I had to come along for Malika's sake." She rubbed her eyes and took a shuddering breath. "I'm okay now. All those feelings when we discovered Malika missing hit me at once."

He grinned. "Wanted to strangle her when you found her, huh?"

"Oh, no. No." How did he know her fear had morphed into anger?

"Don't worry about it. It's natural. Haven't you ever seen a distraught mother reunited with her missing child in the grocery store? The hugs and kisses of relief are soon replaced with finger-shaking and threats." He shrugged. "It's just another expression of fear, guilt and bone-melting relief."

"How'd you get so smart about kids?"

His blue eyes darkened. "I had some experience with my sister's kids until…she cut me off. I haven't seen my niece and nephew in two years."

"Your sister cut you off?" Raven covered her mouth with her hand. "She blames you for the accident that killed your parents?"

"She's not the only one." Buzz slumped back against the headboard and crossed his arms behind his head. "You saw Lance Cooper at the Arapaho yesterday morning."

Raven licked her lips. The mood had certainly shifted in here, as if the cold air from outside had seeped in through the window. It suited her. Guilt piled upon guilt didn't engender lustful thoughts.

But the slabs of hard muscle across Buzz's chest did.

"You want to join me tonight?" He patted the bed beside him.

Just like that?

She needed more seduction than a stark question. She'd already been feeling as if they'd been punished for their attention to each other. In fact, she couldn't figure out how married couples with children ever managed to have sex.

Another good reason to leave the parenting to others.

"I don't think that's a great idea, Buzz—for a lot of reasons."

He shrugged. "We may have different reasons, but I agree with you." He squeezed her hand as she rose from the bed. "Get a good night's sleep."

Raven clicked the bedroom door behind her and leaned her forehead against it. A good night's sleep with peril on both sides of her?

That wasn't going to happen.

BUZZ CRACKED SEVERAL EGGS into a bowl and rinsed the gooey whites from his fingertips in the

sink. He stifled a yawn with his fist and took another gulp of coffee. He hoped the Burumandan
government crushed the rebel uprising quickly,
and his desire had nothing to do with world
peace and everything to do with…his desire. He
couldn't spend many more nights with his ex-fiancée in the bed next door.

He also hoped President Okeke could give him
some information about Jack Coburn. He'd im-
plied that he knew something about the doctor
Jack had been commissioned to rescue. And the
president knew why others were interested in this
doctor.

"What's for breakfast?"

Raven, showered and dressed in her new jeans,
waffle-knit shirt and boots, cruised into the
kitchen and grabbed a mug from the cupboard.
Buzz had never seen Daisy's duds look so stylish
or sexy as they did draping Raven's slim, angular
frame. Her dark eyes with their long lashes didn't
need one bit of makeup.

He dumped the eggs into a frying pan glis-
tening with melted butter. "Scrambled eggs and
I stuck some of that bacon in the microwave. It
looked weird but I'm not big on cooking and I
know you're not."

She wrinkled her nose. "Yeah, but even I
probably wouldn't have gone for the microwave
bacon."

"What do you think Malika eats for breakfast?"

"She'd probably like more burgers and fries. Did you happen to put any fruit into those grocery bags?"

"Bananas." He waved his spatula toward a bowl by the window.

"That'll do." Raven snapped one open and wedged a hip against the counter. "What's on the agenda today?"

"I'll show Malika around the ranch. I'll show you too...if you're interested." Since she was silent, Buzz changed the subject. He didn't want to put her on the spot. "Do you think Malika still wants to see the horses or did she use that as an excuse for sneaking out last night?"

"She mentioned the horses before she fell asleep, so I think she'll be game." Raven tossed the banana peel into the trash and brushed her hands together. "And I'd like a tour of the ranch, too."

Buzz divided the eggs onto three plates and set the timer on the microwave. "You have breakfast duty tomorrow. Your attempts can't be any worse than mine."

"Actually, it smells like real breakfast in here."

"Don't pretend I'm doing a great job just so you can get out of it."

Malika called from upstairs and Raven's cup

jerked in her hand. She hissed as hot coffee splashed her wrist.

"You okay?" Buzz tossed her a damp dish towel.

"I just hope Malika is." She swiped the cloth across the counter and started for the stairs.

"Raven, she sounds fine. Don't overreact to everything."

She rolled her expressive eyes. "Easy for you to say."

Damn. Just when Raven had started to get comfortable in her role as mama, Malika had to split, which gave rise to all of Raven's insecurities and fears. She really believed that Malika's disappearance was somehow related to their lip lock on the sofa. *Okay, more than a lip lock.*

She didn't even know for sure that her parents had been busy making love when her little brother had drowned in the backyard pool. She'd built the story up in her head over the years, convincing herself that her parents' devotion to each other at the expense of their children had resulted in her brother's death.

It had made it easier for her to hate them for their neglect of her without appearing pathetic.

Buzz snorted and shoved a few slices of bread in the toaster. If he had Raven all figured out, how come he hadn't managed to convince her to marry him?

Malika scampered down the stairs with a big smile, all her demons from the previous night exorcised and sent packing. She skidded to a stop on the tile floor of the kitchen and lifted her nose in the air, sniffing.

"At least someone appreciates my microwave bacon." Buzz buttered a slice of toast and dropped it on a plate of eggs and then added the bacon. He crooked his finger. "Follow me."

Malika pranced after him and shimmied onto a chair at the dinette that occupied a bright corner of the big kitchen. She put her napkin in her lap and folded her hands on top of it.

"She has better manners than most pilots I know." He winked at Raven. "Go ahead and eat, Malika. We'll join you in a minute."

Once all three of them were seated, Buzz's gaze traveled around the table. It seemed as if a glow suffused this corner of the room. He hadn't felt warmth like this at the ranch since his parents died.

Shaking his head, he shoveled a forkful of buttery eggs into his mouth. He hadn't taken this job to rehabilitate the ranch or himself. He and Raven had to protect Malika until it was safe for her and her father to return home. And then Raven could return home…to her home.

And then he could return to the friendly skies after he dug up more information about Jack.

About an hour later, he was leading the girls, as he'd secretly begun to call them, around the ranch.

Raven whistled as she surveyed a field of wheat stirring in the chilly wind. "Your manager takes care of all this in your absence?"

"Yeah, Shep Ochoa. He lives on the reservation, but he comes in every day. I heard in town that he and his wife went to visit some relatives for a few days. He'll be back for the rodeo."

"Along with everyone else, I gather."

"Yeah, including a bunch of strangers."

Raven shrugged off her uneasiness and stomped her feet in the dirt. "I'm getting cold out here. I'm going back to the house to get my coat. Do you need anything?"

"I was just getting to the good part. I was going to take Malika to the paddock to visit the horses."

Malika nodded vigorously and slipped her hand in Buzz's. A little sting of jealousy zapped Raven between the eyes. For a girl on edge, Malika showed a lot of trust.

Raven smiled brightly. Best not to get too possessive. She'd have to send Malika back to her father eventually anyway. "Okay. I'll meet you at the paddock, whatever that is."

Rubbing her upper arms, Raven jogged back to the house. She slipped inside and grabbed her coat from the back of the chair and then dropped it. Might as well give Buzz and Malika some time together. Besides, horses scared the spit out of her. She didn't even like the ones plodding around Central Park.

But she didn't want to tell Buzz about her fear. He wanted to teach her how to ride along with Malika. She didn't have the heart to disappoint him—not anymore.

She glided into the kitchen and put a mug of water in the microwave to boil. She'd seen some tea bags in the cupboard but had no idea how old they were. Buzz liked his coffee hot and strong and didn't know Raven had switched to tea.

She and Buzz had split over two years ago, and a lot had changed in that time. She hadn't realized he carried so much guilt over the death of his parents. She'd never seen him unsure of himself before. Doubting himself.

The timer beeped and she plopped the suspicious tea bag into the boiling water. Folding her hands around the warm mug, she stopped in front of the big, stone fireplace and studied the pictures on the mantel.

A breath hitched in her throat at the smiling faces that stared back at her. Which was worse, never having a close family, or having one and then losing it in the blink of an eye?

When she and Buzz had been engaged, he'd been all about family. He couldn't wait to bring her to White Cloud and introduce her to his parents and his sister and her family.

But the idea of family spooked her. She'd been afraid that she wouldn't be able to get Buzz's parents to like her. Her own parents didn't even like her. What chance did she have with someone else's parents?

She sighed and slurped a bit of tea, which tasted exactly like warm water.

Then she froze at the sound of a click behind her. And before she had a chance to turn around and confront this latest intrusion, a woman growled, "If you turn around real slow, I won't blow a hole in your back."

Chapter Eight

The hair on the back of Raven's neck quivered. *A woman.* She and Buzz should've figured a woman would have a hand in snatching Malika. After losing her mother, Malika was a sucker for the kindness of the female sex. Look how quickly Malika had glommed on to Raven?

Raven cleared her throat. "She's not here. We sent her away."

"What the hell are you talking about? Turn around nice and easy, and if you have anything in your hands I'm gonna shoot first and ask questions later."

Biting her lip, Raven extended her arm to the side, her fingers wrapped around the handle of the steaming mug. The woman must be crazy. She didn't want to startle her. "I have a cup of tea."

"Ha! I never heard of a squatter partial to tea. Giving yourself airs, huh?"

Squatter? Maybe the crazy woman was one

of the caretakers. Hadn't Buzz mentioned Shep's wife looking after the house? "Can I turn around now?"

"You'd better but don't try any funny stuff. I'm a good shot."

Holding her arms out to her sides, Raven took little steps until she faced the barrel of a shotgun. The gun looked bigger than the woman gripping it with fierce determination.

She lowered the gun so that it was pointing in the general area of Raven's stomach—a slight improvement. The scowl crumpling the woman's face made her look like an angry elf, with her pixie-short hair and big blue eyes.

Looks could be deceiving.

"Who the hell are you and what are you doing in my house?"

"Y-your house?" The cup nearly slipped from Raven's grip. Maybe Buzz had gotten married for real and had forgotten to mention the fact amid all the excitement.

The man himself suddenly loomed behind the elf. "Josie, put the gun down. Are you nuts?"

Raven nodded. Her assessment of Josie precisely.

Another man appeared beside Buzz and added his voice to the soothing chorus. "Josie, honey, don't be ridiculous. That's Buzz's wife."

Josie pointed the shotgun toward the floor, her

big eyes growing even bigger in her small face. "Buzz's wife?"

"That's right, honey, and they've got a little girl outside playing with our two. Guns and kids don't mix, so put that away." To show her he wasn't fooling around, the man stepped in front of Josie and pried the shotgun from her grasp.

Brave man.

Raven breathed for the first time since Josie opened her mouth. Now she studied the petite woman, whose grim expression had disapproval written all over it. But the disapproval could just as well be for Buzz as for his new bride, since the witch blamed her brother for their parents' deaths.

The thought brought Raven's blood to a slow percolation. How dare this little...person lay a guilt trip on Buzz. Now that Josie had relinquished the shotgun to her husband, Raven clenched her hands and stalked across the room.

"Are you out of your mind? You could've shot me."

Josie folded her arms. "Yeah?"

The man, Buzz's brother-in-law, draped an arm around Josie's shoulders and stuck his hand out toward Raven. "You must be Raven. I'm Austin Yarborough, and this little firecracker is my wife, Josie. Congratulations."

As Raven shook Austin's hand, her gaze met

Buzz's. His shoulder lifted as if to say, *I had to keep our story straight.*

Children's laughter bubbled through the open door, and Raven craned her neck to get a better view. Malika and two other children were playing tag. Raven recognized the kids from the photos on the mantel.

Buzz called the kids inside and invited everyone to have a seat while he retreated to the kitchen to get drinks.

Raven followed him and cornered him at the sink. "What are they doing here?"

"They came for the rodeo." Buzz twisted a cap from a bottle of beer and tossed it on the counter. "That's another obstacle I didn't consider. My sister and her family live in Tulsa. I should've figured they'd come down for the Harvest Festival."

"Why was your sister wandering around on her own? Her husband should keep a tighter leash on her."

Buzz chuckled. "When they drove up, Austin heard the horses and thought he'd find Shep. While she was waiting, Josie saw a shadow in the house, grabbed the shotgun from the truck and went investigating."

"Investigating?" Raven slid some ice cubes in a couple of glasses. "Hunting is more like it. Is she always so tightly strung?"

"That's my sister."

"Has she forgiven you?"

"Does it look like it?"

"She's just wrong…"

Buzz sliced a finger across his throat. "I'm not asking for her forgiveness. Uh, I had to tell them we were married and Malika was our adopted daughter. It's just better if nobody knows the truth."

"I agree." She tipped a pitcher of tea over the two glasses and the ice cubes clinked as the brown liquid flowed around them. "Tea or beer?"

He held up a second bottle. "I could use a beer."

"It's not even noon."

"I could use a beer." He tipped his head toward the family room where the screams of the kids punctuated the low voices of the adults.

"Where are they staying?"

"Here."

One of the sweating glasses almost slipped out of Raven's hand. "I could use a beer, too."

They returned to the family room, carrying the drinks and showing false smiles. Raven placed Josie's glass on the coffee table in front of her and then took a chair across the room.

"What happened to your hot tea?" Josie asked the question as if she were leading an inquisition.

"The iced tea looked better. I think the tea bags were stale."

"Let's cut to the chase." Buzz hunched forward,

hands on his knees. "How long do you plan to stay, Josie?"

"All week, until the end of the Harvest Festival and through Thanksgiving. The kids have the whole week off from school." She took a long swig of her tea and then patted her lips with her fingertips. "Why? I know technically the ranch belongs to you, but Mom and Dad figured I'd always be welcome here."

"That's up to you."

Austin cleared his throat. "The place looks great, Buzz. Shep's doing a good job. I hadn't figured you'd been back much since…"

"I haven't, but I thought it was time to introduce Raven and Malika to White Cloud. And what better time than Harvest Festival?"

"Uncle Buzz?" The little girl had crawled toward Buzz and folded her hands on his knee. "Are you going to teach Malika to ride?"

"I sure am, Britney. Do you want to help me?"

She nodded and stuck her tongue out at her brother. "Wyatt thought Malika was lying."

"Wyatt, that's not nice." Josie nudged her son with her toe. "Apologize to Malika. I'm sure she doesn't tell lies."

Raven slid a glance toward Buzz, but he wasn't biting.

Austin stood up and stretched. "I'm going to get our bags. What room does Malika have?"

Buzz stepped over Britney to grab Austin's bottle. "Malika's in the blue room with the window seat and Raven's in the yellow room."

Patting his pockets, Austin asked, "You're in the yellow room, Buzz? I thought you always took your old room at the end of the hall."

"I am in my old room. Raven's..."

Raven flashed Buzz a look and he realized his blunder, his face reddening to his hairline. Luckily, Austin was too busy looking for his car keys to notice, and Josie was cross-legged on the floor with the kids.

Buzz turned toward the kitchen, saying over his shoulder, "Raven has some of her stuff in the yellow room. She can move it if you and Josie want that room."

"No way." Josie hopped up from the floor. "We're not sleeping next to a couple of newlyweds. We'll take the two rooms on the other end of the hall from you all."

Raven laced her fingers behind her back in an attempt to appear calm. Not only did she have to share a house with her ex-fiancé, now she had to share his bed.

LATER THAT AFTERNOON, the four adults along with the three kids took two cars into town to watch the Harvest Festival take shape.

Raven watched the strangers with their booths

and food stands stream onto White Cloud's main street, and a small knot formed in her stomach. They had passed the rodeo ring just on the outskirts of the town, where huge trucks were already lining the road discharging horses, bulls, assorted cowboys and props.

There had been a tense moment earlier when Josie had asked them the country of Malika's origin. Raven and Buzz had already agreed to stay as close to the truth as possible and had told Josie that Malika came from Burumanda.

Josie had wrinkled her pert nose. "Oh, they're having all kinds of problems over there right now, aren't they? It's a good thing you got her out of the country."

Raven and Buzz had exchanged a worried look and then had hurriedly agreed that they were lucky to have rescued Malika.

Later, when Austin, Josie and the kids were poring over a list of rodeo events, Raven had sidled up to Buzz and whispered. "Don't tell me your sister is a former spy, too. She seems well versed in African politics."

"She's a former high school history teacher. She plans to go back to teaching when the kids are a little older. She knows her stuff."

"Seems like she may have relented in the blame game, too." Raven studied Josie through half-closed eyes. "At least she's speaking to you now."

"For now."

They ate an early dinner consisting mostly of food from the newly constructed booths. The kids plopped down on a curb to share their funnel cake.

Josie shoved her hands in her pockets and chewed on the end of a toothpick. "So how long are you staying in White Cloud, Buzz?"

"At least until the fair's over. Is it okay if we join you for Thanksgiving at the house?"

Josie jerked her thumb at Raven. "She can't cook either?"

Raven rolled her eyes. It seemed as if Josie was transferring her dislike from her brother to her. If that were the case, Raven was happy to take the brunt of her anger.

Buzz jabbed a finger at one of the food trucks trundling down the street. "I think food's on the way for the rodeo and the carnie workers."

"Dad?" Wyatt peered up at his father with a dollop of whipped cream on his nose. "Can we watch them set up the rodeo?"

"I think so. It's on the way back to the ranch, right, Buzz?"

"Yeah."

"Me too." Malika turned a powder-sugared face up to Raven.

Raven dropped a napkin in Malika's lap. "I guess it's unanimous. Will there be horses there?"

Josie snorted. "It's a rodeo. Got yourself a real city girl here, Buzz."

Raven pursed her lips. Wait until little miss country found out Raven had a fear of horses. She'd be all over that. On second thought, she'd better keep that fear to herself.

"I *meant,* are the animals already there?"

Curling his arm around Raven's waist, Buzz pulled her close. "The rodeo opens tomorrow. They have everything they need."

"We should probably get over there." Austin scooped up the messy paper plates and napkins and dropped them into a trash can. "We'll follow you, Buzz."

"More trash." Raven plucked a plastic fork from the ground. Reaching for the lid on the trash can, her hand brushed against the arm of someone else with the same idea. "Sorry."

The hard eyes of Lance Cooper drilled into her, and she stepped back from the malice shooting from his stare.

Buzz was beside her in a flash, taking her arm. He nodded. "Lance."

Lance gripped the edge of the trash can, his knuckles white. "You have a lot to answer for, Richardson."

Josie joined them and hooked her arm through Buzz's. "It's time to stop blaming Buzz for the accident, Lance. Your brother knew what he was doing and if he thought Buzz's plane was safe to fly that day, then it was."

Lance chucked a crumpled paper bag into the trash can, tipped his hat at Josie and turned away.

Josie let out a noisy sigh. "Josh wouldn't want his brother to go on blaming you, Buzz."

Raven rolled back her tense shoulders. Josie's new allegiance to Buzz created a warm spot around Raven's heart, but the woman had no tact at all. Lance had looked ready to strangle Josie... and he'd looked ready to strangle her moments before Buzz's appearance.

Buzz shrugged. "He has his reasons, but I'm not going to let him take out his grief and anger on you, Raven. Steer clear of the guy."

"You don't have to tell me twice."

Ten minutes later, Buzz pulled his truck into a dirt parking lot along with several other vehicles.

"I guess watching the setup is almost as exciting as watching the rodeo." Raven tapped her finger on the glass.

"That's a small town for you."

"It's sweet."

That comment gave him whiplash. Raven ignored his steady gaze. "There's Austin and your sister."

Raven scrambled out of the car, and then helped Malika out of her booster seat. Malika tugged on Raven's hand to loosen her grip.

"Wyatt and Britney are coming this way. You don't need to run over there."

Even though Buzz's sister was a pain, Raven appreciated the kids' company for Malika. She'd brightened up considerably since Wyatt and Britney had come onto the scene. Buzz's niece and nephew were both older than Malika, but Malika was almost as tall as Wyatt.

Austin pointed to the big Ferris wheel scraping the twilight sky. "Are you ready for that, Malika?"

Her eyes grew as big as the wheel and she nodded.

"Let's check out the rodeo before we decide who's ready for what ride." Buzz grabbed Malika's free hand, and he and Raven swung her arms and lifted her off the ground every few steps.

The workers had already constructed the rodeo ring, and now they were busy tightening the fence around the perimeter. Tall bleachers were taking shape on three sides of the ring and huge cranes cast silhouettes on the big sky.

Excitement filled the air, along with some interesting animal smells, and the kids jumped and twirled in anticipation.

Wyatt tugged at his father's sleeve. "Dad, Dad, can we see the horses? They're at the fence."

Several people were scattered along the line of

the fence where some of the rodeo horses whinnied and nickered, nuzzling hands for sweets.

A cold sweat broke out along Raven's hairline as her gaze met the rolling eye of some huge dapple-gray beast.

"Horses. Horses." Malika jumped up and down at Raven's side.

Buzz crouched next to Malika. "I'm going to give you a few rules about how to behave around horses."

Buzz directed his rules to her too, but she was only half listening to his instructions since she had no intention of getting within five feet of that fence. She was just about to make some feeble excuse when her cell phone vibrated in her pocket.

She pulled it out and squinted at the caller ID in the circle of light that beamed from the spotlight fueled by buzzing generators. Her heart thumped against her chest as she read Michael's name on the display—Michael, her date from a few nights ago.

She'd been surprised that he hadn't called her before. Now he was providing her with the means of escaping her dreaded confrontation with those sleek creatures with the big teeth and even bigger hooves.

She held up her phone and wiggled it back and forth. "Phone call. I have to take this."

Buzz glanced at her with a note of worry in his eyes. He must be thinking about that vaguely threatening text message from yesterday.

Raven gave her head a slight shake and mouthed the words *it's okay.*

At least it would be once she got away from those pawing, prancing horses. She punched the talk button. "Hello? Michael?"

If he answered, she couldn't hear him. "Hang on a minute. It's really noisy, and I can't hear you."

Looking up, she headed behind the bleachers with the phone pressed to her ear, almost colliding with a man dressed in a clown suit. This Harvest Festival had everything. As she moved into the shadows cast by the bleachers, the din of the crowd receded, the blur of voices punctuated by a few workmen still securing the rows of seats.

"Michael? I'm so sorry about the other night. I have a good explanation for missing our date."

Yeah, a good explanation that was going to be a total lie.

"Are you there?" She heard his breathing across the line, but he hadn't said a word yet. Maybe he was waiting for the lie. "Michael?"

She held the phone in front of her face to see if the connection had dropped off. A shadow from above fell across her arm, and a chill rippled through her body.

Buzz shouted her name. She jerked her head toward his voice. Out of the corner of her eye, she saw a crane dipping and jerking.

And it was coming straight toward her.

Chapter Nine

The long cable dangling from the crane swung wildly through the air on a direct path for Raven. Buzz dashed toward her and went airborne in his frantic effort to remove her as the crane lurched and plummeted to the ground.

Driving his shoulder into her midsection, he wrapped one arm around her to break her fall. He twisted to the side as they dropped to the ground and hit the dirt with a soft thud. He'd managed to take most of the impact with his own body.

He looked past her shoulder at the cable with a wicked hook on its end tick-tocking above them, the metal catching the light from the scattered spotlights. He blew out a gust of air between clenched teeth, clasping Raven's shuddering body against his chest.

A few of the workmen rushed around the corner of the half-constructed bleachers, cursing at the unsecured crane. One hovered above Buzz and Raven. "Are you okay? I saw the damn thing swing free at about the same time it occurred to me that someone might be in its path."

Buzz stroked Raven's hair. "Are you okay, Raven?"

She shifted her head, which had been buried in his shoulder, and nodded with wide, glassy eyes.

"We're fine." Buzz scrambled to a sitting position, bringing Raven with him. "I think my wife is shaken up."

"I'm sorry." The workman scratched his chin and glanced at the crane. "I don't know how it happened. Nobody was even working that crane."

Another crew member took off his hardhat and mopped his brow with his sleeve. "It must've come loose, boss. Someone didn't secure it in the last go-around."

The boss scowled. "We need to find out who worked it last and pound some sense into his head. Sorry, folks."

Buzz waved them off and pulled Raven into his lap. Her shuddering had subsided but every once in a while, a twitch convulsed her body. Buzz pressed his lips against her temple.

When he'd seen that crane heading for Raven's head, his heart had stopped. He was beginning to believe being out in the field targeting terrorists with Prospero was a safer proposition than anything else. An accident had taken away his parents and one of his best friends. And Raven had been inches away from being another accident victim.

Or maybe not.

He glanced at the crane, dull, mute and innocent in its inactive state. Then he brushed the hair from Raven's face. "What were you doing back here? Taking a phone call?"

She swallowed and ran her tongue along her teeth as if preparing for speech after a long silence. "I answered my cell but I couldn't hear. So I moved back here since it was quieter."

"Who was on the phone?"

In the dim light, her cheeks flushed. "M-Michael, my date from the other night."

His brain was clicking along a single-minded path with no room for jealousy. "You know it was Michael? You spoke to him?"

"Not exactly." She extricated herself from his embrace to look into his face. "But his name popped up on caller I.D. Why are you asking?"

Buzz hooked an arm around her shoulders and staggered to his feet, bringing her with him. He brushed some dirt from her coat. "We're hiding out from some dangerous people…and you almost had a fatal accident."

"You think they're related?" She grabbed the ends of his jacket, blinking her eyes rapidly. "But I was on my own. Malika wasn't even with me."

"You're right."

Her frame stiffened. "Where is Malika?"

"She's getting to know the horses with the others."

Raven plunged her hands into her pockets. "You found me just in time. What made you come back?"

"I turned back to look for you and when I didn't see you, my sixth sense kicked in."

"You sensed I was in danger?"

"I don't know. I just got a weird feeling." He straightened his hat and dusted the dirt from his jeans, feeling foolish under Raven's wide-eyed gaze.

"Well, I'm glad you got that weird feeling. You saved my life, Buzz." She ducked her head to peer through the bleachers. "Are the kids still looking at the horses?"

"Yeah, I don't think they even realized I'd left."

"Good. Don't mention the accident to Malika. She doesn't need anything else to scare her."

"Where's your phone?"

Raven bunched her hands in her pockets, twisting her head from side-to-side. "I must've dropped it."

Buzz bent forward and scanned the ground beneath the bleachers. "Here it is." He plucked it from the dirt and rubbed it against his thigh.

"Let me have it." Raven held out her hand, wiggling her fingers. "I'm going to call Michael. If he didn't think I was a lunatic before, that conversation will seal the deal for him."

Buzz dropped the phone in her palm and watched as she hit a button, holding the cell to her ear. She listened for a moment and then started speaking. "Michael, it's Raven. I'm sorry about the call. We…uh…got disconnected. Try me later and I'll explain about the other night."

"What are you going to tell him?" Buzz raised his brows.

"Don't worry. I'll think of something."

"You always do." He grabbed her arm. "Let's find the others and get out of here."

Malika's high-pitched chatter about the horses formed the background to Buzz's troubled thoughts as he drove home. He'd accepted Raven's assertion that her jilted date had called her. He'd even accepted the work crew's explanation of the wayward crane.

But, damn, he just couldn't shake that sixth sense that warned him something wasn't right.

"I'M READY TO TURN IN." Josie punctuated her announcement with a yawn that took up her entire face.

Raven jumped up to clear the glasses, avoiding Buzz's eyes. She'd done a rush job, clearing her stuff out of the yellow room and depositing it in Buzz's bedroom so that his family wouldn't wonder at a newlywed couple camped out in two different rooms.

But now the moment of truth had rolled around. She and Buzz hadn't even discussed their sleeping arrangements. Too busy dodging runaway cranes.

If she'd had Malika with her she'd be nervous, but there was no reason for a terrorist group to have her in its sights—unless she was protecting Malika. She shivered as she lined up the glasses in the dishwasher.

Buzz came up behind her and whispered in her ear. "Are you ready for bed too?"

She flushed and the glass nearly slipped from her wet hand. She didn't understand her shyness. It wasn't as if she hadn't shared this man's bed before, hadn't peeked at his magnificent naked body, hadn't explored every inch of him.

"Buzz?"

At Josie's voice, the two of them jumped like they shared a guilty secret. Actually, they shared a few of those.

Buzz turned. "Yeah?"

Josie stood on tiptoes and kissed her brother's cheek. "I'm glad you're here."

"Me too." Buzz chucked her under the chin.

Raven smiled as she poured some dishwashing liquid into the little receptacle. At least some good had come out of this nightmare.

When Austin and Josie had trudged up the stairs, Raven snapped the lid of the dishwasher shut and leaned against it. "Looks like your sister forgives you, or at least has realized how ridiculous it was to blame you in the first place."

Buzz smashed a soda can with one hand and then chucked it into the recycling bin. "Glad someone has realized it."

"If Josie has come to her senses, why can't you?" She ran a hand down the tense muscles of his back. "It was an accident, Buzz. The plane malfunctioned. Just like that crane today."

"Yeah, the crane." Buzz shifted toward her, rubbing the stubble sprinkled across his chin.

"Wait a minute. You still think the accident was suspicious?"

"I think everything's suspicious, Raven. You're not accident-prone. Why now?"

"If you're trying to give me the creeps, you're doing a great job." She hugged herself, and Buzz replaced her arms with his own strong set.

"I don't want to scare you, but we need to be vigilant at all times. Farouk and his cohorts want to get their hands on Malika. The little girl is as good as gold to them. If they have her, they can make Okeke do anything they want, including turning over the mechanism to weaponize the virus."

"You just said it. They want Malika, not me."

"Maybe they want to get rid of one more layer between them and the girl."

Raven coughed out a laugh from her dry throat. "I'm a layer now?"

"I'm sorry." Buzz cupped her face in his hands and laid a quick kiss on her mouth. "Let's get some sleep."

Sleep? Not with the promise of that kiss still burning on her lips. She wanted him and to hell with the consequences. Having Austin and Josie here eased her worries. A second set of parents represented insurance against failure. And Austin and Josie were the real deal, not fakes.

Buzz left the downstairs hall light burning while Raven floated into her new room. She hadn't bothered buying pajamas for herself at Daisy's. Now that oversight presented a problem. If she climbed into Buzz's bed naked, she'd be way too obvious.

He stopped at the bedroom door, slouching against the doorjamb. "Do you want me to sleep on the sofa in the family room? I can always pretend I fell asleep in front of the TV."

"No. Unless you want to fall asleep in front of the T.V."

"Nope."

"Um, could I use one of your T-shirts or something for pajamas?" She waved her hand at the closet doors.

"Knock yourself out. Do you want to take a shower first? I'm going to take one after rolling around in the dirt after that crane malfunction."

Shower? Was that code word for planning sex?

"Yeah, I'll take a quick shower." Raven opened his dresser drawer and plucked a white T-shirt from the neat stack. Clutching it to her chest, she slipped into the attached bathroom.

She secured her hair and stepped into the shower. Three minutes later, squeaky clean, she toweled off and brushed her teeth. She'd soaped up and rinsed off like the Energizer Bunny in case Buzz changed his mind and packed off downstairs. But on second thought, if she'd taken longer, maybe he would've joined her.

She dropped the T-shirt over her head, surprised at the fresh scent. Buzz kept a supply of clothes at the ranch, but she didn't expect them to be freshly laundered.

Bunching her dirty clothes in her arms, she opened the bathroom door and peered around the edge. Buzz looked up from his book.

"That was fast. Knowing how long you usually take in the bathroom, I was settling in for a good, long wait."

She stuck out her tongue. "Some things do change."

"That's good to hear." He snapped his book

shut and slid off the bed. "That T-shirt looks a lot better on you than me."

Raven stared at the bathroom door after he'd closed it behind him. Her gaze tracked to the chair in the corner. Should she pretend maidenly modesty and claim the chair?

She blew out a puff of air. She wasn't a maiden and she wasn't modest. Why pretend now?

She peeled back the covers on the bed and slipped between the sheets. Leaning over, she plugged in her cell phone charger and then plumped the pillows behind her. She didn't have a book or even a magazine from downstairs, so she picked up Buzz's book—a political thriller. Didn't he get enough of that in real life?

She thumbed through the pages and jumped when Buzz swung open the bathroom door. Wisps of steam curled around his body as he stepped into the room, a towel hanging low on his hips. His biceps bunched as he reached up and sluiced back his hair.

Raven's belly fluttered and she squeezed her thighs together. He looked like a page from a calendar—hot pilots. Maybe Mr. November.

He raised one eyebrow at her snuggled in his bed. She chewed on her lower lip. Maybe she should've bunked in the chair.

"Did you lose my place?"

"Huh?"

"In my book." He pointed to the forgotten tome in her hands. "Did you lose my place?"

She held up the book and flicked the card he'd used as a bookmark. "No. You're at the place where he finds the dead body."

"Really?" He turned and placed his palms on the dresser, hunching forward to look into the mirror. "I thought I was at the place he has sex with his hot accomplice."

His towel slipped an inch down his backside and Raven's fingertips tingled at the thought of running her hands across his hard muscles. She drummed her fingers on the book's cover. "If you can't remember, the sex scenes must not be very good."

"I prefer doing, not reading."

Raven dropped the book. Well, he sure cleared that up. She patted the space beside her on the bed. "Are you going to do me or are you taking the chair?"

She gasped and covered her mouth with both hands. Did she just ask him if he was going to *do* her?

Buzz laughed. "The chair? You gave yourself away with that Freudian slip. Besides, the minute you told me you didn't want me sleeping on the sofa, I knew what you wanted."

He did? She hadn't been quite sure herself, but leave it to a man to see everything in black and white. If they were sharing a bed, it was a done deal.

He whipped off the towel and tossed it onto the chair. At least that chair had served some good purpose. She studied his form, drinking in all the familiar ridges and dips, and he let her. He could've been a marble statue positioned for her enjoyment.

But he was flesh and blood and the finest male specimen she'd ever had the pleasure of pleasuring.

He approached the bed slowly. He grabbed the book and tossed it onto the nightstand. Kneeling on the bed, he yanked the covers off her body.

Goosebumps raced across her flesh and her nipples hardened against the soft cotton of the T-shirt in anticipation of his touch. He straddled her and curled his fingers along the hem of the shirt.

"You don't need this anymore."

She opened her eyes wide. "You mean you want it back already?"

Bunching the material in his hands he yanked, and the T-shirt ripped right up the middle. She gasped. "You really didn't like that T-shirt, did you?"

"I didn't appreciate that it kept me from this." He placed his index finger at the base of her throat and began tracing a line down her body. He ended at the elastic waist of her panties.

"Oh no, you don't." She grabbed his hand. "I have a limited supply of these."

He leaned over her, his erection skimming her belly, and placed a finger on her lips. "I'll be careful."

Sitting back on his heels, he wedged two fingers on either side of the elastic. When his warm fingers made contact with her hips, she jerked.

Buzz dipped his head and gripped the waistband with his teeth, tugging lightly. Sucking in a breath, Raven tipped up her pelvis. He dragged her panties down as his hair tickled her belly and his nose skimmed across her sensitive skin.

He got them as far as her thighs, and then looked up with a satisfied grin. "Pretty talented, huh?"

"You can use your hands for the rest."

Buzz pulled off her panties with a flourish. He ran his palms along the outsides of her thighs until they curved in at her waist. Splaying his hands on her ribcage, he tickled the underside of her breasts with his thumbs.

Raven skimmed her fingers through his short hair, pulling his head toward her breasts. He didn't need much encouragement. His warm lips puckered around one nipple, drawing it into his mouth.

Raven arched her back to make contact with his erection. She rubbed herself against his hardness and hooked one leg around his muscular thigh.

The dull ache of wanting that had carved a hole in the pit of her stomach since the day she left him flared into a hot, demanding need. She cried out hoarsely, "Take me."

He kissed her neck, her ear and finally her lips. As his tongue invaded her mouth, he parted her thighs and entered her with a desire that matched her own. She wrapped her legs around his hips and rode him, sucking his tongue and digging her nails into his buttocks, wanting him closer still.

With each thrust, he created a seal between them. She reached a shattering climax, its shifting pieces stabbing her with new delight at different points in her body.

Just when she thought she'd wrung out every drop of pleasure from her orgasm, Buzz exploded inside her and the pleasure turned into a deep, abiding contentment.

Still inside her, he braced himself on his forearms and kissed her nose. "I'm glad some things don't change."

Her eyelashes fluttered. "Oh, I don't know. That was better than I remembered it."

He tugged the torn T-shirt around her. "Do you want to keep this on?"

Her eyelids flew open. "I have to keep something on. What if Malika calls for me in the middle of the night?"

"What did you have on last night?"

"Not even a torn T-shirt."

"Then what's different about tonight? If she calls out, grab another T-shirt. I have plenty that aren't ripped."

"But I... But we..." She stammered to a stop. They'd just made love. That was the difference. Couldn't a child always tell when her parents' attention lay elsewhere? She could.

He bounded from the bed. "I tell you what. I'll get another shirt, a bigger one, and put it at the foot of the bed. That way, if she calls you'll be ready."

"Okay." She slid back against the pillows. She jerked her head toward the nightstand when her charging phone buzzed. It must still be on.

"What's that noise?" Buzz tossed another T-shirt onto the foot of the bed.

"It's my phone." She grabbed it by the charger and swung it into her lap. "Caller unknown."

Buzz perched on her side of the bed, his body suddenly tense. "Answer it."

"Are you crazy? We just made love. We're kind of in the middle of something here."

"Take the call, Raven."

She studied his serious face for a moment and then punched the call button. "Hello?"

Michael's voice rushed over the line, filled with relief. "It's great to hear your voice live, Raven."

"Michael?" Signaling to Buzz, she drew her brows together. "What do you mean, live?"

"I got your voicemail from earlier, but I didn't pick it up until a few minutes ago. Your message made no sense at all. Where are you anyway?"

"Why didn't you understand my message? You called and we got disconnected." She met Buzz's eyes and shrugged.

He whispered, "Speaker," and she pushed the button without hesitation. She had nothing to hide, and the muscle ticking in Buzz's clenched jaw didn't look like jealousy.

"That's the thing, Raven. I never called you."

Her pulse ramped up and she licked her lips. "Now you're not making sense, Michael. I got a call earlier this evening and your caller ID popped up. We tried a conversation but…the call dropped. I called you back and got your voice-mail."

"Raven, the strangest thing happened the night of our date. I mean stranger than your not being home when I went to pick you up. I rang your bell outside a few times, and then Jenny Baker, you know the woman on the fifth floor?"

"Yeah, yeah." Raven forced the words out as her lungs felt depleted of air.

"Jenny let me in. I noticed a guy lounging near the elevators, but didn't think anything of it at the time. Then I banged on your door a few times and took off when you didn't respond."

"Did you try to call me?"

"That's the weird part. I went outside and walked up the street for a bit to catch a cab. When I fumbled in my pocket for my cell, some guy came up behind me and whacked me on the back of the head."

Raven choked and met Buzz's blazing blue eyes. "A-are you okay?"

"I'm fine, but the dude who attacked me, and I'm sure it's the same guy who was in your apartment building, stole my wallet and my cell phone."

"Your cell phone?"

"Yeah, isn't that odd? Maybe he took it because I had it out and he was afraid I'd call the cops when I came to or something. Anyway, what I'm trying to tell you, Raven, is that I got your message because I dialed into my voicemail from my landline. I didn't call you before because your number was in my cell phone. When I got your message, I went through a few hoops to get your cell number."

"You never called me?"

"That's what I'm telling you. The person who called you earlier from my phone is probably the guy who mugged me."

Chapter Ten

The phone slid from Raven's hand. With the blood pounding behind his temples, Buzz scooped up the phone from the bed and held it out to Raven in his cupped hand. He whispered, "Keep talking."

"Raven?"

She cleared her throat. "The guy who stole your phone called me? Creepy. Why would he do that?"

Buzz massaged the back of his neck. He could think of several reasons.

"I have no idea. Maybe he just went through my contacts and called all the women. Are you okay? I heard about some ruckus at the U.N. and thought about you. Were you involved in that?"

"Oh, no. That was just some false alarm." She closed her eyes and pinched the bridge of her nose. "I'm sorry about the date, and I'm especially sorry about the mugging outside my building. My boss called me away on a special assignment and I'll be out of town for a while. It was all rush-rush."

"Maybe another time then. Just wanted to make sure you were okay with all the strange happenings. And if that dude calls you again, tell him I still have a headache and to return my damned phone."

Raven managed a short laugh although her face was stiff with worry. When she ended the call, she pressed the phone against her chest. "What does it mean, Buzz?"

He folded back the covers and pulled her down next to him, encircling her with his arms. With her back molded against his chest, he rested his cheek against her hair. He didn't want to scare her, but she already knew the truth.

"I think someone was watching your place. When Michael showed up for your date and knocked on your door, that someone followed him, mugged him and took his phone. He then used it to call you. It's probably how they got your number the first time they texted you with that warning from the disposable phone."

A tremble coursed through her frame and Buzz hugged her tighter.

"But the crane. That had to be an accident. It's just a coincidence I got that call at the same time."

He couldn't take her down that path any more

tonight. He wouldn't give voice to his wild speculations. Instead he nuzzled her soft ear and murmured. "Sure, babe. The crane was a coincidence."

THE NEXT MORNING, BUZZ REACHED across the cold sheets to pull Raven close again. She'd slept curled up against him all night and he wanted more. But his hands clutched at emptiness.

The noise from the shower meant she hadn't been up long, but it also meant she was ready to start her day and had moved beyond tangled sheets and warm kisses.

Unless he joined her in the shower.

He swung his legs over the side of the bed, and the shower stopped. It worked like a splash of cold water on his face…and other areas farther south. He'd better not get too invested this time. He wanted one lifestyle and she wanted something completely different. They couldn't see eye-to-eye before and not much had changed…except Raven had saved the life of a little girl and that little girl had come to love her and depend on her. Was it enough to change Raven?

The bathroom door inched open, and Buzz called out. "It's okay. I'm awake."

She poked her wet head into the room and puckered her lips into an O. "Did I wake you?

You looked so peaceful. I didn't want to disturb you."

"No, you didn't wake me up." He jerked his head toward the bedroom door. "Is anyone else up and about?"

She toweled her hair and replied in a muffled voice. "I've been hearing some clinks and clanks that sound like breakfast. Does your sister cook?"

"Yeah, she does. She's not such a bad addition to the household after all."

"I'm glad the two of you are talking again. What's on the agenda for today?"

Raven retreated into the bathroom and then sauntered into the bedroom, running her fingers through her black locks.

Buzz suffered a stab of disappointment when he took in her fully clothed body. Even if their expectations for the future veered in different directions, he could go for more of what they'd shared last night in the here and now.

"The kids will want to go back to the festival. Josie will probably want to do some riding, and I might get Malika on a pony. You too?"

"Buzz." She sat on the foot of the bed and pulled on one of her boots. "Why are we avoiding the obvious?"

Blood rushed to all the right places and his toes curled into the rug. Maybe she could go for some here and now, too.

"I mean, some terrorist who's trying to kidnap Malika mugged my friend and stole his cell phone to call me."

Second splash of cold water this morning.

Buzz scratched his chin. It's not as if he'd forgotten about the danger, but damn, having sex with your beautiful ex-fiancée while on an assignment was a major distraction.

"So Farouk knows your name, knows where you live and mugged your date. It doesn't mean he knows where you are now or even that you have Malika."

He'd been the one spouting doom and gloom last night, and now he was trying to put a good spin on it. A good night's sleep and the light of day could do a lot toward banishing paranoia.

Raven dropped her other boot with a thud. "You think Farouk is after me?"

"Whoa." He shifted toward her and massaged the back of her neck. "Nobody is after you. They want Malika. You're of no interest to them without her. And Farouk wouldn't stake out your apartment or mug Michael. He'd send his henchmen for that."

Her neck stiffened beneath his fingers and she twisted her head around. "Henchmen?"

"Associates."

"You said henchmen." She stuffed her foot into

her boot and stomped her feet when she stood up. "Maybe we need to get out of White Cloud."

Buzz pushed off the bed, dragging the sheet with him. The time for naked bodies had long since passed. "My agreement with President Okeke includes White Cloud and White Cloud only."

"But if we can't keep her safe here?"

Did Raven doubt his abilities to protect Malika? He tucked the sheet around his waist and squared his shoulders, trying for a little dignity. "I'll keep her safe. We can't go dragging President Okeke's daughter all over the country without his knowledge or approval. What if something happens to her on the road?"

Raven flattened her palms against his bare chest, sending another shaft of desire through his core. "Okay, I trust you, Buzz. Now I'm going downstairs to see what your sister whipped up for breakfast."

She planted a chaste kiss on his lips and scurried out of the bedroom as if she feared that kiss would lead to an all-out conflagration. If only.

After he showered and dressed, Buzz perched on the arm of the chair and called Colonel Scripps. If he couldn't contact President Okeke and he wouldn't contact the CIA, the colonel had to be his lifeline to the outside world.

As usual, the colonel picked up on the first

ring. He could be playing golf, watching a movie or having sex with his wife and the colonel always answered after one ring from any former Prospero team member. Must've been hell on his wife all those years.

Colonel Scripps's gruff voice rolled over the line. "Is the package safe?"

By *package,* he must mean Malika, and Buzz's nerve endings tingled. Had somebody compromised the colonel's phone line? Maybe he couldn't talk freely.

"Yes. There have been certain...complications."

"Complications? There typically are."

After the colonel assured him the line was still secure, Buzz recounted the situation with Michael and his cell phone. He didn't mention the crane.

Colonel Scripps cursed. "I can't believe you dragged Raven along."

A flash of heat claimed Buzz's body and he took a deep breath before responding. "It's not like I had a choice, sir. The little girl had gotten attached to Raven."

"A child attached to Raven Pierre?" Colonel Scripps snorted. "I can't picture that. President Okeke's daughter might have more to fear from Raven if she happens to sully one of her expensive suits than from these lunatics chasing her."

An image of Malika wiping one of her pow-dered-sugared hands on Raven's jeans stamped itself on Buzz's brain and he smiled.

"Raven saved the girl's life. They have a bond."

"If you say so, Buzz. The president is still in hiding. Government forces in Burumanda have a tentative hold on the capital, but the rebels have control of some outlying areas. It's not safe for President Okeke to return, and it's certainly not safe for his daughter."

"Is the president showing any signs of weak-ening to the terrorists' demands to turn over the weaponry for the virus?"

The colonel grunted. "Not to us."

"Then why doesn't he turn it over to us and let us worry about either destroying it or securing it?"

"The capability to weaponize a virus is power, and the president wants to hold on to that power."

"Do you think Jack might've stumbled onto some evidence that President Okeke had plans for himself?"

"I don't know, Buzz." The colonel released a heavy sigh. "If Jack's not dead, why hasn't he contacted one of us? If he's imprisoned, why is Farouk looking for him? None of it makes sense."

"I'm hoping when this is all over, President Okeke can give me some information about Jack.

When I return his daughter to him, he'll feel obliged to repay me."

"I hope you're right. In the meantime, let's hope the new Burumandan government can crush the rebels and keep the weapons of terror out of their hands."

The colonel ended the call and Buzz shoved his cell phone into the pocket of his jeans. The breakfast smells from the kitchen had been curling their way upstairs for the past fifteen minutes, and his stomach had been in major revolt.

He jogged down the stairs and turned the corner into the kitchen. Three sets of eyes skewered him.

"Everything okay?"

He detected a sharp edge to Raven's voice and noticed Josie's quick glance between the two of them. He swooped into the kitchen, wrapped his arms around Raven and kissed her. Might as well take advantage of the charade.

"Everything's fine. Had to take a call about my schedule." He popped a piece of bacon into his mouth and rolled his eyes. "Much better than my sorry attempts at cooking."

"I made pancakes, eggs, bacon and toast. I even sprinkled a few chocolate chips on the pancakes for the kids." Josie dusted her hands together.

"Those were for the kids?" Austin wiped his

mouth with a napkin and grinned. "You'd better make a few more of those, honey."

"Where are the kids?" Buzz tried to disguise the edge to his own voice.

Josie waved her hands. "Relax, new daddy. The kids are out front playing. Malika has been chattering all morning about horses, so I hope you intend to put her on a pony before we go into town."

"I'm going to do that right after breakfast." He ruffled Raven's soft hair. "Are you ready for your lessons?"

"You don't ride, Raven?" Josie flipped a few pancakes and then grabbed a handful of chocolate chips.

"No. I'm a city girl, never spent much time around horses."

Josie narrowed her eyes. "Yeah, I remember. You and Buzz were engaged before, but none of us ever got a chance to meet you. Then you...you two broke it off."

Smiling brightly, Raven dug her fingernails into Buzz's arm. "Then we realized our mistake and got back together."

"Funny, Buzz never mentioned that part."

"Uh, you weren't exactly speaking to me, Josie."

Josie reddened beneath her freckles. "Okay.

You got me there. I realized my mistake too, Buzz."

He reached over and tugged a lock of her sandy-brown hair. "I'm glad."

Austin gathered the kids and herded them in for breakfast where they played a noisy game of counting the chocolate chips in their pancakes.

Buzz surveyed the scene and the pretense of it left a bittersweet taste on his tongue. Mom and Dad had always envisioned just such a scene for this house—their two children married with kids of their own.

Now Mom and Dad were dead and the woman sitting across from him was a fake wife. He stabbed another pancake with his fork and plopped it on his plate.

He'd take her any way he could get her.

RAVEN PROPPED ONE BOOTED FOOT on the fence and leaned her chin on her folded arms. Malika had no fear. She sat atop that giant beast, even if everyone had assured her it was a pony, with a grin that claimed half her face.

"Scared, huh?" Josie hopped on the fence beside her.

"What?"

"You're afraid of horses, aren't you?"

"It's that obvious?"

Lifting her shoulders, Josie turned her attention to her brother leading Malika around the paddock. "You didn't come with us last night when we went to see the rodeo horses, and I can tell you're hoping Malika's lesson will run into your time."

"You got me."

"Why'd you break off the engagement with my brother? He didn't say much. Never does. But I could tell you broke his heart."

Raven raised her head and gripped the fence. "Maybe I did break his heart, but then you stomped on it when you blamed him for the plane crash that killed your parents."

Josie's bottom lip trembled. "I was hurting. I lashed out."

"Buzz was hurting too, and he was already blaming himself."

"I know it's not Buzz's fault, but he would've been piloting that plane instead of his friend Josh if he hadn't rushed off on that last-minute assignment." She fixed Raven with a watery stare. "He went on that mission because of you. To forget about the breakup."

"Oh, for heaven's sake." Raven shook the fence back and forth and Josie wobbled with it. "Now you're going to blame *me* for your parents' deaths? Can't you accept that it was an accident?"

A tear rolled down Josie's cheek. "It was an accident that could've been prevented. Equipment failure caused it. I can't help believing if

Buzz had been flying his own plane, he would've checked it out more thoroughly."

"His friend was an experienced pilot. I don't think Buzz would've done anything differently, except if he'd been piloting the plane he'd be dead now, too."

Josie hopped down from the fence and wiped her face with her sleeve. "I don't blame Buzz anymore."

She then stalked into the paddock, leaving Raven hanging on the fence. Good thing that woman wasn't really her sister-in-law.

Raven had played her cards right. A few hours later, after everyone had determined Buzz didn't have time to give Raven a riding lesson, they drove into town to check out the progress of the Harvest Festival, which was set to officially open this afternoon.

As she strolled down the main street of White Cloud hand-in-hand with Buzz and Malika, Raven kept a tight grip on Malika until the girl was practically struggling to escape. Loud noises caused Raven to jump and she steered clear of construction materials being used to build the last of the booths.

And this was White Cloud. She wouldn't have lasted two minutes in New York under this kind of pressure. A chill trickled down her spine when she wondered what would have happened had she not accompanied Buzz and Malika that night. Would the man who mugged Michael have done worse to her?

More of the booths had opened, and the adults sauntered after the kids as they shot ahead to check out each display. Buzz hadn't been kidding when he said the Harvest Festival drew a crowd.

Britney and Malika dragged the adults to a craft booth for corn dollies.

Raven scanned the tables littered with dried stalks and bits of cloth. "What the heck is a corn dolly?"

"It's a doll made out of corn husks." Britney pinched a doll by one arm and swung it in front of Raven's nose. "Don't you know anything, Aunt Raven?"

Flicking a lock of hair over her shoulder, Raven said, "I buy all *my* dolls at FAO Schwarz."

The ploy and the attitude didn't work.

With her nose in the air, Britney sniffed. "Who'd want to buy a doll when you can make a corn dolly?"

"If you can't beat 'em, join 'em." Raven winked at Malika and straddled the bench to make her very own corn dolly. Not that she particularly excelled at arts and crafts.

Wyatt had no interest in corn dollies and

kept asking his father when the parade of rodeo clowns was coming through town.

"What exactly is a rodeo clown?" Raven lodged her tongue in the corner of her mouth as she tied off the head of her doll. "I saw a clown last night and wondered what he had to do with a Harvest Festival and a rodeo."

Buzz clicked his tongue. "During the bull riding event, the rodeo clown distracts the bull when the rider has jumped or fallen off. Instead of going for the cowboy, the bull charges at the rodeo clown, who's wearing bright colors and attracting the bull's attention."

"Even though I find all clowns creepy, that sounds like a dangerous job." She held up her corn dolly. "Not bad, huh?"

"I'll bet it's better than any old doll from FO Shorts." Britney tweaked the doll's hat into place.

"It's… Never mind." Raven dropped her doll when a loud horn blared from the end of the street.

"It's the parade!" Wyatt scrambled toward the curb. "Let's get a good place."

Josie stayed with the girls, who wanted to finish their corn dollies, so Raven and Buzz trailed after Wyatt and his father, who jostled for position at the curb.

Since Buzz towered over Austin, he stood behind him while Raven placed her hands on Wyatt's shoulders and peered over his head. Cymbals and buzzers joined the horns in a general cacophony that preceded a parade of horses, calves and clowns. Lots of clowns.

The rodeo clowns created a blur of color and motion as they tumbled down the street, walking on their hands, standing on each other's shoulders, spinning on their heads. Raven could understand a poor bull going crazy after getting a load of these guys.

She'd never liked clowns as a kid and liked them even less as an adult. Foolishly, as the clowns drew closer, she dropped one hand from Wyatt's shoulder and slipped it through Buzz's arm.

Most of the people bunched on the sidewalk were laughing at their antics, and occasionally a clown would run into the crowd and draw one of the onlookers into the street. Raven shrank against Buzz's shoulder to make herself look smaller while she recited in her head, "Not me, not me."

One short clown with the traditional bulbous red nose and white pancake makeup scanned the crowd as he somersaulted down the street. His eye caught Raven's and she mumbled a curse under her breath.

Sure enough, when the clown drew level with her, he jumped in the air, touching the toes of his huge shoes and then shoved his face so close to Raven's his phony nose almost touched hers.

Gasping, she drew back sharply from the face with its smile painted-on. Through the clown's grimace, he hissed, "Be careful."

Chapter Eleven

Then the clown disappeared. The people around Raven laughed good-naturedly at her shock, not realizing her surprise was a result of the clown's words, not his deeds.

She clutched Buzz's arm. "Did you hear that? Did you hear what the clown said?"

Buzz looked down at her with smiling eyes that quickly sobered. "Are you okay? Did he accidentally hurt you or something?"

"H-he said something to me. Didn't you hear it?"

"Are you serious? Did the clown proposition you or something?" Buzz tilted his head and ran a thumb across her cheek.

She stamped her foot and shook his arm. "No. Buzz, he told me to *be careful*."

He jerked his head in the direction of the receding parade. "Are you sure?"

"I heard him. He was in my face and then whispered, be careful."

"He whispered?" Buzz had turned back to her and now his eyebrows had disappeared under his cowboy hat. "You heard a whisper above all this noise?"

"You don't believe me?"

He smoothed his fingers down her arms and caught her agitated hands in his. "I'm just trying to make sense out of it, Raven. How did you hear a whisper?"

"Didn't you see him?" She snatched a hand from his and pointed down the street. "He was in my face. His nose practically touched mine. Of course I heard him."

A few people in the dispersing crowd glanced at her with sidelong looks. She closed her eyes and scooped in a lungful of air.

"Buzz, maybe they're here. Maybe they tracked us down. Maybe one of them is that creepy clown."

"Would you recognize him again if you saw him?"

"God, I don't know." She covered her face with her hands. "He had a big red nose and white face makeup. He was short. I don't know. He was a clown."

Cupping her elbow, he led her back to the corn dolly crafts table.

Wyatt danced around the table where the girls were still working. "You should've seen it. A rodeo clown picked Aunt Raven out of the crowd and blew an airhorn in her face."

Josie smirked. "You must've enjoyed that."

"Can I help it if clowns are naturally attracted to me?" Raven shrugged and relaxed the lines out of her face. She couldn't have Josie believe both horses *and* clowns terrified her.

Buzz ducked his head and murmured in her ear. "We're going to the rodeo tonight. See if you can pick him out, and I'll have a talk with him."

Raven nodded and then almost immediately felt foolish. That rodeo clown had been a tumbler and an acrobat. What were the chances that some terrorist could jump in and impersonate a rodeo clown? The idea was ludicrous and a smile tugged on her lips.

"What now?"

"I don't know, Buzz. Maybe I imagined the whole thing."

He pushed his hat back on his head. "You seemed awfully sure of yourself ten minutes ago. Why would you imagine a clown telling you to be careful?"

"Maybe he said something else. Maybe he said *be cheerful* or something like that."

"Really?" His eyes widened.

"You said it yourself. It was noisy and chaotic." She sidled closer to him. "Besides, don't you think it would be an incredible coincidence for a terrorist to step into the shoes of a clown?"

"I don't know." He draped an arm across her shoulders. "Was this particular clown that skilled?"

"He was vaulting over horses, walking on his hands and doing handsprings. I can't do that, can you?"

"Nope. Do you think you might've just fixated on him and when he approached you your mind started merging one fear with another?"

"Fear? Oh, you remember my distaste for clowns, huh?" She giggled and a little tension seeped from her shoulders.

"How can I forget? I had to convince you there wouldn't be one Bozo in sight when I took you to that acrobatic circus."

Holding her stomach, she doubled over with laughter. "I remember."

"What's the matter with Raven? Is she having post-clown stress disorder?" Josie had both girls by the hands and an evil grin on her face.

Raven straightened up and wiped the tears from her eyes. Even Josie's snarky comments couldn't dampen the relief she felt after dismissing her paranoia. She held out her hand. "Let me see your corn dolly, Malika."

As Raven exclaimed over Malika's pretty doll, Buzz tucked an arm around her waist and pulled her to his side. Then he said, "We're still going to find that clown tonight."

THE COLORED LIGHTS OF THE carnival rides shifted and blended like a kaleidoscope while the screams of the rides' occupants ebbed and flowed. Raven and Buzz had taken Malika on the Ferris wheel and while Malika squeezed her eyes shut as they swooped forward, Raven found herself studying the crowd below.

Ever since Buzz had stated his intention of locating the rodeo clown who had singled her out, an underlying dread had been creeping into her system. She wanted to forget about her encounter with the clown. She'd dismissed it as a product of her overactive imagination and stress.

Apparently, Buzz hadn't found her story of the doom-saying clown as unbelievable as he'd pretended.

Buzz bumped her shoulder with his. "Are you having fun?"

"Except for that spinning ride, I'm hanging in there. Don't make me go on the spinning ride again."

He laughed. "I don't think Malika cared for that ride either."

"Buzz." She tucked her hand in his fleece-lined pocket. "We don't have to seek out that rodeo clown. I'm almost positive now I imagined his words."

"It can't hurt to check it out. We can start by thanking him for the entertaining parade and see where it goes from there. See if he acts suspiciously or repeats the warning."

"See if he swings another crane at my head?"

His hand joined hers and the strength of his fingers as they curled around hers loosened the knot of tension in her belly. "Is that what you're worried about? If he were responsible for the crane incident, he wouldn't be drawing attention to that fact.

"And let's face it." He slid a glance to Malika, pinching puffs of pink cotton candy from a beehive of the stuff. "If the people who want Malika are in White Cloud, they'll want to conceal themselves for as long as possible."

His words acted like a prod, and Raven spun around and charged back to Malika's side. She stroked her hair as if to make sure the little girl was still in one piece.

As Malika held out her cone of spun sugar, Raven nipped off a dollop of cotton candy and stuffed it in her mouth. The gauzy texture melted in sweetness on her tongue, almost drowning out the bitter taste of fear Buzz's words had sent skittering across her flesh.

If the rodeo clown had cautioned *her* to be careful, what did that mean for Malika?

A voice from the loudspeaker announced the start of the rodeo and much of the crowd milling around the carnival rides surged toward the rodeo ring.

Buzz scooped up Malika in his arms and placed a hand on the curve of Raven's back to guide her through the human traffic. He leaned forward, stirring her hair with his breath. "When you see the rodeo clown, point him out to me."

They climbed the bleachers to a spot near the top and scooted down the cold metal benches. Austin and Josie sat in front of them with their kids bouncing in place and twisting around to point out the intricacies of the rodeo to Malika.

An announcer took the center of the ring, welcoming everyone to the Harvest Festival and rodeo. While she stood for the national anthem, Raven surveyed the rodeo personnel for a glimpse of the clown from the parade. Who knew all clowns looked alike?

She shook her head at Buzz and they sat down to watch the roping event. While Wyatt and Britney squealed and clapped, Malika tugged on Raven's sleeve. "Is that hurting the cow?"

"I don't think so." She rubbed Malika's back. "Let's ask Buzz-Daddy."

Once Buzz assured Malika that the roping

didn't hurt the calves, she squealed as loudly as the other two kids.

Raven clapped and cheered at the cowboys' exploits, waiting for the bull riding and a better look at the rodeo clowns. For a break in the action, the announcer invited all kids between the ages of five and ten to come down to the ring for a contest. The object of the contest was to snatch a ribbon from the tail of a scampering calf, and all the kids in their party clamored to try their luck.

Raven grabbed Buzz's arm. "Do you think we should let her?"

"Nothing's going to happen with a crowd of people watching. She'll be fine."

Raven reluctantly released Malika's hand as Austin guided the kids down to the ring. A few of the clowns gathered around the edges of the ring, but they all looked too tall to be the one who might have spoken to Raven.

Maybe the parade clowns were different from the actual rodeo clowns. Maybe the man was wearing street clothes now. Maybe he was watching her.

Folding her arms, Raven squinted at one end of the ring where the kids were lining up. "Do you see Malika, Britney and Wyatt?"

"You can see Malika's red jacket." Buzz put an arm around her shoulders and pointed. "Josie loaned her one of Britney's jackets. She thought it was odd that Malika had only a dressy coat with her."

Raven plucked at the cashmere coat she'd been wearing on the escape from New York. "She probably thinks my coat is weird too, paired with jeans and sweatshirts."

"I told her it was a spur of the moment trip."

"Did she buy that?"

"Not really."

"So Josie senses something's off?" Raven rolled her eyes. "She should've been the covert ops agent in the family."

"She knows better than to question me... even about a hasty marriage." He jerked his chin toward the rodeo ring. "Watch. They're ready to go."

A calf with a red ribbon tied to its tail scampered into the ring. A loud horn blasted and the kids took off after the calf. Raven spotted Malika tearing after the calf with her arms outstretched.

Tears flooded her eyes and the kids and the lights blurred. She sniffed, wondering when she'd grown so sentimental.

Buzz turned a smiling face toward her with brows raised. "Are you okay?"

"I'm just thinking how far removed this is from rebel soldiers rampaging through her house and assassination attempts on her father."

He kissed her temple. "That's why we're here. To get her away from all that."

And had they? Raven's heart skipped a beat when the race ended and several rodeo clowns flooded the ring to lead the kids to the exits. With a dry mouth, she studied the man who ushered Wyatt, Britney and Malika out of the ring, and then realized the clown was a woman.

The kids returned to their seats grumbling about pushing and shoving and how they all had a chance at the ribbon except for some kind of sabotage from another contestant. When the cowboys returned to the ring for a few rope tricks, Raven excused herself.

"I'm going to brave one of the Porta-Potties and get something to drink. Does anyone want anything?"

Buzz jumped up. "I'll come with you." He lifted Malika from her seat and plopped her in the middle of Wyatt and Britney. "Tell her what's going on, you two."

Raven scooted past the knees and purses and waited for Buzz in the aisle. When he joined her, she said, "You didn't have to come with me. I don't plan on standing beneath any more cranes."

"I didn't think you could carry back all that popcorn on your own." He jumped from the bleachers and lifted her to the ground.

While Buzz stood in line at the concession

stand, Raven wandered back to the carnival grounds to the row of blue Porta-Potties on the side of the property. Two lines had formed to use the johns and Raven blinked when she saw a rodeo clown at the front of one of the lines.

Her heart pounded as she joined the back of the line, taking note of the clown's bright green shirt under his baggy polka-dotted overalls. His short stature confirmed her identification of him as the clown from the parade.

She slipped out of line when the clown entered the next available Porta-Potty and waited in the shadow of an oak tree. She glanced over her shoulder at the concession stand, which partially concealed the line snaking into it. If she waited for Buzz to get through the line and ran to get him, the clown might disappear.

She had to do this alone.

The door of the Porta-Potty swung open and the man emerged, adjusting the straps of his overalls.

Raven stepped from the shadows into his path. "Excuse me?"

He jerked his head up. As his gaze focused on her face, his eyes widened, their roundness exaggerated by the makeup encircling them. His gait faltered but he kept moving, putting his head down, the curly red hair of his wig flapping at his ears.

"Excuse me." Raven put out a hand. "W-weren't you the clown who approached me during the parade?"

His head shook, the red fright wig whipping back and forth. "Don't know what you're talking about, lady."

Raven drew her brows together, certain this was the same man who singled her out in the crowd. "The parade through Main Street. You came up to me."

He scurried faster, glancing to his right and left. "Came up to a lot of people during the parade. Enjoy the rodeo."

Raven scuffed her feet to a stop. She wasn't about to go chasing him into the rodeo ring, but his odd behavior convinced her he *was* the clown who had approached her.

And he *had* whispered the warning.

She turned the corner of the concession stand just as Buzz was coming away from the window, his arms laden with bags of popcorn and his hands clutching red licorice.

"Where have you been? Long lines?"

She relieved him of a few bags of popcorn and stuck a piece of licorice in her mouth. "I found the rodeo clown."

Buzz almost dropped the remaining bags of popcorn. "You did? Where is he?"

"Probably back at the rodeo." She waved her

licorice toward the lights of the rodeo ring. "I spoke to him."

This time, Buzz jerked and fluffy kernels of popcorn jumped from the tops of the bags. "You talked to him?"

"Yeah, and now I'm more convinced than ever that he told me to be careful. He was acting weird. If he'd just acknowledged that he'd come up to me during the parade, I might have doubted his words. But he didn't want to talk to me."

"Well, I want to talk to him."

"I think you're going to have to wait." A roar from the rodeo ring signaled a new event. "Come on. I'll point him out."

They edged up the steps of the bleachers, balancing the snacks and slid into their seats. Malika clambered over the row in front to wedge herself between Raven and Buzz. "Bull riding."

"That's right." Buzz handed her a piece of licorice. "The cowboys are going to try to ride the bulls for as long as they can."

Wrinkling her nose, Malika chomped on the licorice. "Will they get hurt?"

"When the bull tosses them or they fall off, the rodeo clowns make a lot of commotion to distract the bull away from the cowboy."

Schooled on the finer points of bull riding, Malika leaned her elbows on Austin's shoulders to get a better look.

Buzz nudged Raven. "Do you see him?"

"Two posts down from the gate where the crowd is crushing in. The guy in the lime-green shirt."

"Can't miss him. I'll pay him a visit after the show."

The first bull rider came charging out of the gate, his arm waving in the air as the bull bucked and twisted. The cowboy slid to the side of the bull and tumbled off, rolling toward the fence. A barrel with a clown waving his arms and legs from the sides rolled across the bull's vision. The bull lowered and gored the barrel once before the clown scampered out of the ring.

During the display, Raven's fingers had curled around the strap of her purse. Once the rider and the clown were safe, she flexed her fingers and took a deep breath.

The next bull rider shot out of the gate like a cannon. The bull kicked up his back legs and thrashed his shaggy head from side to side. Still the cowboy clung on, his hat flying off his head and his chaps flapping around his legs. The bull seemed to give one last monumental heave, which sent the rider sailing through the air. He landed on his back and scrambled to his feet.

Another clown sallied into the ring—a short clown with a lime-green shirt. He waved his arms and flapped his baggy overalls before abruptly dropping his arms to his sides.

The bull pawed the ground and switched his attention from the prone cowboy to the spectacle of the clown. The clown staggered backward and swayed to one side as if in slow motion. The crowd exhaled a collective gasp at the clown's bravery…or stupidity…by not hightailing it out of the ring.

"What's he doing?" Buzz sat forward in his seat.

Shaking his massive head, the bull focused on the clown, who was now clutching his chest and weaving his way toward the gate. Two more clowns jumped into the ring, but the bull had his target.

The bull charged. He head-butted the clown, snagging him with his horns as screams and shouts rose from the audience.

Before Raven covered her eyes with a shaky hand, she caught a glimpse of bright green stained with red soaring through the air.

Chapter Twelve

A wave of shock reverberated through the crowd, and Buzz crushed Malika against his chest. Raven had planted her forehead against his shoulder.

"That was bad. The guy's not moving." Austin twisted in his seat.

The cowboys had herded the bull from the ring, and a couple of people were crouching beside the injured rodeo clown. Raven's rodeo clown.

Raven raised her face to his, and her dark eyes shimmered with confusion. "What just happened?"

If Buzz hadn't seen the man attacked by a bull, he'd be making some strange connections right now between the clown's injuries and his warning to Raven. He skimmed a hand down her throat. "It's just an accident. He couldn't or wouldn't get out of the way. Maybe he thought he needed to put on a better show."

Britney had climbed into her father's lap and Austin shook his head. "That was quite a show."

"God, he's still not moving." Josie had to drag Wyatt's attention from the ring. "I think we should get going. They're not going to carry on now, will they?"

"Depends on how badly he's injured." Austin's words merged with the wail of a siren, and an ambulance pulled onto the rodeo grounds.

Many people had vacated their seats and surged toward the parking lot while others milled around, wondering if the show would go on.

"The kids are upset. We should leave." Josie grabbed Wyatt's hand and shuffled past her husband toward the aisle.

Worry gnawed at Buzz's gut, and the ashen pallor of Raven's face told him the same thoughts were running through her mind. Why that particular rodeo clown?

They packed up the kids and headed for their cars. Buzz exchanged meaningful glances with Raven on the ride home but since the drive was short and Malika showed no inclination to fall asleep, he kept his thoughts to himself.

Once they got the kids to bed, Buzz wanted nothing more than to retreat to his bedroom to discuss the accident with Raven, but Josie had other plans.

She rummaged in a kitchen drawer and pulled

out a corkscrew. "Anyone else want to join me? If ever a night called for it, I think this one qualifies."

"Count me in, honey." Austin collapsed on the sofa. "It's not like we haven't see accidents at rodeos before. Stuff happens."

"Yeah, but usually there's some sign of life from the injured person." She held up a wineglass. "Raven? Buzz?"

Raven said, "Sure. Let me help you."

Buzz tried to catch her eye while she hung up her coat in the closet in the foyer, but she avoided his gaze and joined Josie in the kitchen.

Maybe she didn't want to discuss the implications of the rodeo accident. Maybe he didn't either. He propped up his feet on the coffee table, folding his arms behind his head.

When Raven handed him a glass of wine, he smiled his thanks and gestured to the cushion beside him. "That wasn't the best introduction to a rodeo for you."

"Or Malika." Raven traced the rim of her wineglass with her finger and turned toward Josie. "Are kids traumatized by this sort of thing?"

"Kids are resilient. I swear I wanted to get out of there more for my sake than Wyatt's. But it depends on the kid. Is Malika particularly sensitive? Did she have a hard life before you and Buzz... adopted her?"

Raven bent forward to brush an imaginary piece of lint from her sweater. "Well, she didn't have a typical middle-class American upbringing."

You can say that again. Buzz took a swig from his wineglass. Compared to what Malika had witnessed in her short life, a bull goring a rodeo clown was small potatoes. Still, the girl had to be on edge, sensitive to the slightest upheaval in what was supposed to be her safe haven.

Josie narrowed her eyes above her glass. "What were the circumstances of her upbringing? You two never did go into much detail about how you came to adopt Malika, and I've learned never to ask my brother a direct question."

Buzz clinked his wineglass onto the table and stretched. "That's a long story for another night. I'm going to go up and read. Raven?"

It wasn't a question so much as a command. His sister would pry and dig and ferret until she got to the truth. And he didn't want to reveal anything until he got Malika safely back in the arms of her father and installed back home in a secure country.

And he sure as hell didn't want to come clean about his bogus marriage. He wanted to live that lie as long as possible.

"I'll join you." Raven pinched the rim of his

glass and hers between two fingers and headed for the kitchen.

He waited by the foot of the stairs as she washed the glasses in the sink. He didn't want to leave her alone with Josie for one minute.

As they said their good-nights, Josie's speculating face assured Buzz he'd removed Raven from the line of fire just in time.

Buzz snapped shut the bedroom door behind them and leaned against it. "So what do you think?"

"I think she's on to us." Raven fell across the bed, drawing her knees to her chest.

"Not Josie." Buzz folded his arms across his chest and dug a shoulder into the door. "I'm talking about the accident."

"It *was* an accident." Clasping her arms around her legs, she rocked forward. "How could it be anything but? Are you trying to tell me someone slipped the bull an energy drink or something to make him angry? I gather bulls act that way all the time."

Buzz studied the tips of his boots. "But did you notice the clown? I can tell you, rodeo clowns do *not* act that way all the time."

"The staggering and flopping around?" She rested her head on her knees. "I thought that was part of his act."

"It may have been, but when that bull started

charging, the guy should've been hightailing it to the fence."

"What are you saying? You think there was something wrong with him before he entered the ring?"

Buzz pushed off the door, raking his hands across his scalp. "I don't know. It just seems like too much of a coincidence. The guy acts nervous talking to you and fifteen minutes later he has an accident in the ring."

"You told me yourself—rodeo clown is a dangerous job."

"So is this." He sank onto the bed next to her and covered her clasped hands with one of his. "Maybe it's time for you to go home."

"No. I can't leave...Malika. Can't you see? She means a lot to me."

He traced the hills and valleys of her fingers. "You don't have to prove anything, Raven."

"Prove anything?" She froze, her mouth forming a thin line.

"You know, prove you can like kids. Prove you can be a mother when it's something you'd rejected for years, when it's the reason you called off our engagement."

She flung her hands up, dislodging his grip. Her dark eyes flashed with fire and her cheeks reddened as if scorched by the flame.

"That's what you think I'm doing here? Using

Malika for some sort of redemption?" Her nostrils flared. "Or do you think I'm using her to get to you? You think you're so freakin' irresistible, I'm using a child to get you back into my bed?"

Buzz gestured toward the bed with a slight smile. "It worked, didn't it?"

Her jaw dropped, and Buzz tensed his muscles, preparing for a slap or a punch to the gut. *Come on, Raven. I can take it. Get it over with and then get the hell out of White Cloud. Go back home. Go back to safety.*

The line of her jaw hardened and she clenched her hands. "Bryan Richardson, you're an ass."

Then she rolled from the bed and slammed into the bathroom.

He collapsed on the mattress. She didn't say she wanted to leave, but how long would her anger allow her to stay with him? In danger?

The running water in the bathroom seemed to go on forever, and then she burst through the door. "I'm taking the bed. You can have that comfortable chair over there or sleep downstairs. I'll leave it to you to explain to your nosy sister."

Grinning, he eased back against a pillow. "Did I say I minded being back in your bed? I admire your tenacity. You're a brilliant strategist."

"And you're an ass. Get out."

He'd definitely be getting out. He wouldn't be able to sleep in that chair while the woman he loved had this big bed all to herself. He couldn't give up Raven any more than he could give up breathing.

He shrugged and slid from the bed, grabbing a pillow. He had no intention of sleeping downstairs on the couch. He had a perfectly good guest room down the hall—but she didn't need to know that. Might as well send her back to New York with a little guilt niggling at her conscience. Just in case.

He crept down the hall and slipped into a vacant room. The cold, empty sheets enveloped his body and he punched a pillow. Did he really think Raven would come running back to his arms once he'd finished this assignment and found Jack?

She'd done it this time. Was twice too much to expect?

THE FOLLOWING MORNING, Raven brushed her teeth so vigorously she almost wore off the enamel. She hunched over the sink and studied the dark circles under her eyes. The blissful cloak of sleep hadn't stolen over her much last night because of Buzz's words churning through her mind.

She should've socked him when she had the chance.

She soaked a washcloth in cold water and

pressed the cloth to her eyes. She didn't want Buzz to notice the remnants of a sleepless night.

She tossed the wet cloth into the tub and started applying the cheap drugstore makeup she'd bought the other day. The concealer gave her the appearance of a clown and she wiped it off with a tissue.

Clown. She crumpled the tissue in her hand and her knuckles turned as white as the porcelain sink. That had to have been an accident. One of life's little coincidences. Maybe the rodeo clown's encounter with her outside of the porta-johns shook him up.

But why would her questions shake him up if he hadn't said anything to her in the first place? And why had he warned her?

She didn't care. Buzz was right about one thing. She needed to go home. She didn't fit in here at White Cloud with horses and rodeos and corn dollies. And kids.

A tap on the bedroom door lured her away from the mirror and the mess of trying to hide her sleep-deprived eyes. If that was Buzz trying to get his stuff, he'd just have to wait.

Another thing he'd been right about—she found him irresistible.

She swung open the door with discontent twisting her features only to find Malika on the threshold.

"I am going to be a pea."

"You have to pee?"

Malika giggled. "I am going to be a pea in the parade."

Oh damn, another parade. Just what she wanted to see.

Raven pasted a bright smile on her face and widened her eyes. "You are? What parade is this?"

"The Harvest Festival parade." Josie leaned against the doorjamb, her bright-blue eyes scanning Raven from head to toe. "I hope you don't mind. The city has vegetable costumes and the kids dress up and march down Main Street."

"And you want to be a pea?" Raven tickled Malika behind the ear.

"Or a carrot."

"Just don't be a Brussels sprout." Screwing up her face, Raven stuck out her tongue.

Malika skipped out of the room singing, "No Brussels sprouts, no Brussels sprouts."

Josie tipped her head to one side and Raven prepared for the onslaught.

"You're good with her."

"You seem surprised." Raven bit her tongue. She should've just accepted the compliment.

"Well, we'd heard that's why you ended things with Buzz. He wanted kids. You didn't. Sort of surprising you show up here with a ready-made family."

"People change."

"Yeah." Josie's gaze tracked down Raven's sweater and jeans, settling on her low-heeled boots—the only shoes she had besides her Jimmy Choo stilettos tossed in the closet.

"We'd also heard you were a city girl through and through, from a wealthy family, boarding schools, designer clothes, the whole nine yards." She smirked. "That's a football reference."

"Yeah, thanks. Harvard has a football team."

Josie's eyes lit up. She liked to needle and seemed to enjoy getting needled back almost as much. "I think the Sooners kicked their butts once."

"Probably."

"You and Buzz must've been in a real hurry then if you couldn't even be bothered to pack a Louis Vuitton with your designer duds." She waved a hand over Raven's ensemble. "Unless Daisy's set up shop in Manhattan."

"We were in a hurry. If you want to know why, ask Buzz." Raven pushed past Josie, restraining an impulse to slug another Richardson.

Raven had the kitchen to herself and zeroed in on some pancakes cooling on the counter. She stuck her fork into a couple and dropped them on her plate. Josie irritated her but at least the woman could cook.

Carrying her plate in one hand and a bottle of maple syrup in another, Raven wandered to the kitchen table and peered out the window. Buzz had the kids doing chores.

Did he really think she'd been using Malika to rehabilitate her image? She sawed into a pancake and popped a bite into her mouth. The sweet syrup was at odds with the sour taste in her mouth. Maybe she should go home, let Buzz deal with this mission in his own way. Forget she'd ever seen Buzz. Forget they'd ever made love.

She dropped her fork and took a gulp of orange juice. Like that would be easy to forget. After they split up, it had taken her months just to forget the taste of him on her lips.

The front door swung open and Raven jumped. Austin barreled into the room, whistling some country song. "I saw Buzz with the kids, but where's Josie?"

Raven pointed her fork at the ceiling. "She's upstairs."

"Sounds like you want to keep her there."

Raven shrugged. She liked Austin and really didn't want to get into a discussion with him about his wife.

He laughed. "Yeah, Josie's little but she's like a tornado. Don't let her get to you. She likes you."

Raven swallowed and kept her mouth shut. Austin was delusional.

"Hey, I was in town this morning and got some news about the rodeo clown."

"Is he okay?"

Austin ran a hand across his mouth. "No, he's dead."

Raven's heart skipped a beat. "Is the rodeo canceled?"

"They're not going to cancel the rodeo. It's too bad about the guy, but it wasn't the rodeo. Seems he had a heart attack."

"A heart attack?" Raven wrapped her hands around her glass of juice. "But he was a young man."

"Was he? How could you tell under that makeup and from that distance?"

"I—I just assumed because of his line of work."

Austin spread his hands. "I don't know how old he was, but if he had heart disease even a young man can die of a heart attack. Anyway, it wasn't the bull's fault and they're not going to cancel the rodeo."

"I guess that's good for the kids. What time is this parade of vegetables?"

"After lunch." He paused on the first step of the

stairs. "I hope you don't mind that Josie and the kids and I barged in on your retreat here and are dragging you to the Harvest Festival every day."

"Not at all." *Well, maybe except for Josie.* "It's fun for Malika."

"Malika's school must have this Thanksgiving week off from school, too. She's in kindergarten, right?"

Raven stared at him while her brain whirred around ages and grades in school. Five. Kindergarten. Right. "Yes, yes, she's in kindergarten but we don't have her enrolled in school yet."

Austin blinked. "That's probably a good idea to give her time to get acclimated. Burumanda, right?"

"Huh?"

"Buzz told us she came from the area that formed the new country recently."

"That's right. Her parents died in the upheaval." She chewed the inside of her cheek. Was that too much information? Apparently, she didn't know what Buzz had told them.

"Sad story. She's lucky to have you." Austin's voice echoed down as he trod up the stairs.

Was she?

For the rest of the morning, Raven watched Buzz with the kids. Wyatt and Britney were already competent riders and Malika wanted to match them.

Raven hung on the fence, calling out encouragement. She and Buzz hadn't spoken directly to each other since their argument last night. Did he believe her words of support for Malika were an act?

Buzz led Malika's horse to the fence. "She's doing great."

"I can tell." Raven backed up two steps.

"Don't be afraid of the horse, Mama."

Raven slid a glance toward Buzz as the customary lump formed in her throat when Malika used that word. Did he think that was fake?

"Okay, you teach me how not be afraid."

Malika leaned forward on the pony, hugging his neck. "Put out your hand slowly."

Raven stretched out her hand toward the pony's nose.

"Bunch up your hand and let Star sniff you."

"His name is Star?" Raven fisted her hand and held it in front of Star's big, snuffling nostrils.

"Buzz-Daddy, give Mama a piece of apple for Star. Star likes apples."

Buzz withdrew an apple from the pocket of his jacket and handed it to Raven. "Watch his teeth."

Raven put the apple under Star's nose and held her breath as the horse pulled back his lips and took it with his teeth. He demolished the apple in a few bites and nuzzled Raven's hand.

"See? He likes you, Mama. He trusts you. They need to trust."

Raven flashed a dark glance at Buzz. Horses *and* people needed to trust.

When they were alone together in the car with Malika in the backseat, Buzz turned to Raven. "You know the rodeo clown died from a heart attack?"

"Austin told me. Is that good news or bad news?"

"It's bad news for the rodeo clown either way, and it's bad news for us, too." His jaw formed a grim line.

Raven glanced in the backseat and shook her head at Buzz. Malika didn't need bad news, whether she understood their conversation or not.

When they met Austin and Josie at the festival information booth, Josie herded the kids to the dressing room to find veggie costumes.

Raven hooked an arm around Buzz's and dragged him toward a food stand. "Okay, why is a heart attack bad news for us?"

Buzz shoved his hands in his pockets and widened his stance. "I'm not sure you need to know, Raven. I think you should leave. I can send you back to Tulsa with Austin and Josie and you can catch a flight out from there."

Grinding her teeth, Raven blew out a harsh breath. "I'm not leaving Malika, and I don't care if you think it's an act because if you do think it's an act, I'm certainly not interested in renewing our relationship so that should prove it's not an act."

Buzz raised one eyebrow in a look that she hated because it was so sexy, and she didn't want to find him sexy right now.

"Do you want to say that again so I can understand it?"

"No." She poked him in the chest. "Now what's the matter with having a heart attack, besides the obvious?"

He ran a hand along the rim of his hat. "There are ways of inducing a heart attack in someone, ways that make the attack appear natural."

She whistled. "So you think someone did that to the clown? But why? Why was he warning me?" She grabbed Buzz's shirt as an image slammed against her brain. "He was there by the crane."

"What?"

"The other night, when I took what I thought was Michael's call. I saw a clown by the bleachers. I bet it was the one who warned me."

"Do you think he saw who released that crane?" Deep grooves etched lines in Buzz's face. "That means it wasn't an accident."

"Th-that also means Farouk tracked us to White Cloud." Raven glanced over her shoulder as if she expected Farouk to appear in the flesh. "How, Buzz? Nobody outside that room at the hotel even knew you were involved with President Okeke and even the people in that room don't know about White Cloud."

"There are always ways, Raven." He rubbed his chin and scuffed the toe of his boot into the ground.

"We need to get Malika out of here."

"I'll work on it."

"There's still something that doesn't make sense. Suppose somebody did kill that rodeo clown because he witnessed the crane accident and tried to warn me. But why would someone come after me? I didn't even have Malika with me at the time."

"I don't know." Buzz jerked his chin toward Josie hustling the kids out of the costume area. "We'd better help out. All I can think of is with you out of the way, there's a clearer path to Malika."

Raven strode toward the kids, calling over her shoulder, "Not if I have anything to do with it."

The girls were struggling into their costumes and Malika peered at Raven through the face of a pea pod. Britney danced around in her carrot costume, bobbing her head to wave the leaves at the top, and Wyatt sulked as a stalk of wheat.

"I don't know why I have to be in the parade. It's for girls."

"You do it every year, and besides, you have to show Malika the ropes." Josie pulled his arm through the beige sleeve and grimaced. "Boys. When you and Buzz have another, you should stick with girls."

Raven ignored Josie's comment and flipped the mesh screens over the face cutouts on the girls' costumes. "These are cute. What exactly do you do in the parade?"

"Stupid dancing, and I'm not dancing." Wyatt folded his arms across his chest.

Josie flicked his head with her finger. "Oh for goodness' sakes, Wyatt, lighten up."

Buzz whispered in Raven's ear, "I don't blame him. I wouldn't want to go dancing down the street as a stalk of wheat either."

"Time to line up." Josie grabbed the girls' hands as Wyatt trailed behind, dragging his feet.

"I have to pee." Wyatt dug his sneakers into the ground.

Josie's face turned red and her eyes glittered. The sight had a strangely comforting effect on Raven. Good parents got angry and frustrated with their kids, too.

"I'll take him." Raven held out her hand to Wyatt. "Do you want to hold my hand? That costume looks like it could throw you off balance."

He put his slightly sticky hand in hers and she didn't even mind. "We'll meet you in the lineup for the parade."

The festival organizers had set up Porta-Potties in a parking lot and Raven headed toward them, gripping Wyatt's hand. He wriggled loose and pointed to a small café. "I can go in there. We know the owners. They'll let me."

"Okay. If you say so." Raven pushed open the door to the crowded café and stopped a waitress. "Bathrooms?"

"There's a unisex in the back to the right, but you have to buy something."

So much for having friends in high places.

Placing her hands on Wyatt's shoulders, Raven steered him toward the small hallway in the back of the restaurant. "It's back there. I'm going to buy a drink. Meet me right here."

She watched him walk to the hallway, and then she turned toward the counter. "I'll have an iced tea to go, please."

After she paid, she shoved the straw through the lid and sauntered to a table facing the back hallway. She leaned against the table and watched the single bathroom door.

A blonde woman swinging her purse at her side hurried into the hallway and pushed open the bathroom door.

The straw slipped out of Raven's mouth. The

waitress had told her the café had a single bathroom. She pushed off the table and crept down the hallway. A brisk breeze blew strands of her hair across her face. She peeked around the corner of the hallway. A back door stood open, leaving a screen door rattling in the wind.

Pinpoints pricked her flesh, and Raven turned back to the bathroom door. She tried the handle.

"Occupied." A woman's voice sang out from behind the door.

A spiral of fear snacked up Raven's spine. If the blonde was in the bathroom alone, where was Wyatt?

Chapter Thirteen

The blood rushed to Raven's head and she grabbed the door handle to steady herself. With the other hand, she banged on the door. "Wyatt?"

"I told you, it's occupied. Do I sound like Wyatt?"

Raven slapped the door with both palms. "Is there a little boy in there? Did you see a little boy come out?"

Her head twisted wildly back toward the dining room.

The door burst open and the blonde poked her head out. "There was nobody in here and I didn't see anyone leave."

A pulse pounded in Raven's temples as she rushed into the dining room. She asked a few people if they'd seen a boy in a wheat stalk costume but nobody had seen Wyatt.

Raven stumbled back into the hallway and careened around the corner to stare at the open back door. Wyatt didn't want to be in the parade. He probably slipped out the back to avoid the humiliation of marching down the street in a wheat getup.

He was hiding from her. That's all. Kids did that sort of thing all the time, didn't they?

With shaking hands, Raven pushed on the screen door handle and staggered into the alleyway behind the restaurant. She ran to the end of the alley and called out. "Wyatt!"

Drumbeats signaled the beginning of the parade and people surged onto the sidewalk with their cameras raised. Raven whipped her head from side to side, the drumbeats matching her pounding heart. She tripped over people, pushing them out of the way as she scanned the children in costume for a glimpse of Wyatt.

She lost a child. She lost a child.

She wouldn't make any better parent than her own mother and father. She should have never gotten a drink at the counter. Wyatt was gone because of her selfishness.

Buffeting against the edge of the crowd, Raven studied the perimeter of the parade. If someone had taken him, they'd be headed for a car right now. She dashed into the street, the colors and motion making her dizzy.

She couldn't do this alone. She'd have to go back to the others and admit that she'd lost Wyatt, that he'd disappeared under her watch. That she'd failed.

Wiping her clammy palms on her jeans, she crossed over to the sidewalk where Josie, Austin and Buzz had lined up to watch the parade. The costumed children had almost drawn even with them. They'd soon discover that Wyatt wasn't with them. Or her.

She tripped over the curb and grabbed Buzz's arm. "Buzz."

"There they are." He pointed to a row of vegetables clapping to the beat of the drum and chanting something about harvest time and Thanksgiving.

"Buzz."

"Look at Malika." He gripped her shoulders and turned her, pressing her back against his chest.

She saw the pea pod skipping down the street with the carrot and the stalk of wheat on either side of her. The stalk of wheat?

She called out. "Wyatt?"

The costumed child turned and lifted his hand. Raven slumped against Buzz, grateful for his solid chest otherwise she'd have sunk to the ground with relief. He must've gone out the back door to take a shortcut to the parade.

"Are you okay?" Buzz balanced his chin on top of her head and she nodded.

As the last of the kids wound around the corner, the parade broke up and the participants wended their way through the crowd to find their parents.

Malika, Britney and Wyatt ran up to the adults, the mesh over their faces pulled back. The girls giggled and chatted about the parade while Wyatt hung back, silent and watchful.

Raven had no intention of hiding what happened. She tugged at Wyatt's costume. "What happened to you at the restaurant?"

Josie jerked her head around. "What do you mean?"

"I took Wyatt into that small café at the end of the block to use the bathroom and he took off out the back door."

Wyatt shot her a look filled with conflicting emotions. Did he think she wouldn't tell his mother to protect herself?

"Wyatt! You know better than that. You must've given Raven a scare."

He kicked the ground. "I didn't want to be in the stupid parade."

His mother patted his shoulder. "I'm glad you decided to join after all, but you need to apologize to Raven for running off like that."

"I—I didn't decide to join the parade." Wyatt continued studying the toe of his sneaker. "He made me."

"Who made you? Dad?" Josie glanced at Austin, but he lifted his shoulders.

"No, some man outside the bathroom."

The fog that had rolled in when she'd discovered Wyatt missing encased Raven's brain again. She shifted her stance toward Buzz and met his eyes briefly.

Two lines formed between Josie's brows. "What man?"

"I dunno. Some man grabbed me when I left the bathroom and carried me out the back door."

Josie sucked in a sharp breath and dug her fingers into Wyatt's shoulder. "He grabbed you?"

"Who was it? Where is he?" Austin had put both arms around Britney as if he expected the man to come back and grab her, too.

"I dunno. I didn't see him. He grabbed me sideways, like under his arm. I kicked my legs, but I couldn't yell because he put his hand over my mouth and I had this stupid costume over my face."

Josie gave a strangled cry and covered her own mouth. "What did he do, Wyatt?"

"He carried me out the back door and started running. I tried to get away and I was able to yell. Once I yelled, he stopped running, and asked me my name."

"You didn't tell him?" Two red spots had formed on Josie's cheeks.

"Yeah. I told him my name was Wyatt, and he said you guys sent him to take me back to the parade. Then he let me go and I joined the parade to get away from him."

"Austin?" Josie had drawn Wyatt into her embrace, her freckles standing out on her white face.

"Of course I didn't tell anyone to get Wyatt. Raven, did you see anything?"

Raven cleared her dry throat. "I'm sorry. I sent Wyatt to the bathroom and then went to the counter to get a drink. When I went back to the bathroom, he was already gone. I checked in the alley, but the man must've let him go by that time."

"That's the craziest thing I've ever heard. Did you know him from before, Wyatt?"

"I didn't see him."

Austin clapped his hands. "I think the kids did a great job in the parade and deserve a treat."

When Josie had taken the kids to a candy apple booth, Austin turned to Buzz. "Buzz, should we notify the police?"

"It can't hurt. I know Sheriff Tallant. If strangers are running around picking up kids, he'd want to know about it."

"Maybe he knew Wyatt, and Wyatt just couldn't place his voice. Josie and the kids are well known around here." Austin scratched his chin and cast a hopeful glance at Buzz.

"But why would someone grab him like that?

The person would have to know Wyatt wasn't in the restaurant by himself." Raven had placed her hand on Buzz's arm, her animosity toward him forgotten for the moment.

"I don't know. But why grab a kid and then drop him? Too much trouble? Too many people around?" Austin had curled his hands into fists.

Raven bit her nail and shot a glance at Buzz. *Grabbed the wrong kid?*

Buzz clapped Austin on the shoulder. "Why don't you get the kids home? They could probably use a nap before the bonfire tonight anyway. Raven and I will talk to Sheriff Tallant. Who knows? Maybe there have been other incidents."

Austin smacked a fist into his palm. "What's happening to this world? Kids aren't even safe at a small-town festival?"

Raven and Buzz walked the others to the car, and the sight of the shotgun in the back window gave Raven a warm feeling.

They watched them drive off, and Buzz turned to Raven. "What do you think?"

"I think the people who are after Malika are here. They saw me with Wyatt dressed in his costume and figured I had Malika with me. The bathroom visit gave them the opportunity they'd been waiting for...and who knows how long they've been waiting."

Buzz pulled on his earlobe and swore under his

breath. "I think you're right. Once the guy realized he had a boy on his hands instead of the expected girl, he dropped him."

"It's a good thing." Raven shivered and hugged herself. "What if he figured he could use Wyatt to get at Malika?"

"Maybe they don't want to make it that complicated."

"As if it's not complicated enough. We need to get Malika out of White Cloud. Isn't there some way you can contact President Okeke? Your plane's at the local airport. Let's just take off."

"We might just have to do that—whatever the consequences." He took her arm. "Let's go report this to Doug Tallant."

The craggy-faced sheriff looked as though he'd stepped right out of a Western. He greeted Buzz by pumping his hand and smacking him on the back.

"I'm glad you stopped by again and with your pretty new wife." He winked at Raven and Buzz introduced them. Raven tensed her muscles in case he wanted to smack her on the back, too. He didn't.

Raven explained to him what had happened to Wyatt, and Buzz asked if there had been any other similar incidents reported. When he answered in the negative, it didn't surprise Raven.

She knew Wyatt's abductor had been targeting Malika.

Sheriff Tallant lifted his hat and ran a hand through his shaggy gray hair. "We've never had any trouble like that at the Harvest Festival, Buzz. I'd hate to think we're attracting the wrong kind of people, but when you get a lot of strangers swarming into town there's bound to be a bad apple or two."

"Let me know if you get any other complaints, Sheriff."

"I sure will. This is shaping up to be one eventful festival."

"Oh?" Buzz gripped the rim of his hat, raising his brows.

"The rodeo clown. He had a heart attack, you know. Have never seen a cowboy die in the ring before, even if it was from natural causes."

"Yeah, natural causes." Buzz shook the sheriff's hand. "Thanks, Sheriff. Maybe your deputies can be on the lookout for any suspicious men talking to kids."

"They always are, Buzz. They always are."

Raven shoved her hands in her pockets once they stepped outside. "So Wyatt's the only kid who was grabbed and then almost immediately deposited."

"It could be random."

"Maybe if that was the only out-of-the-ordinary

occurrence at this festival, but a crane almost fell on my head and the rodeo clown who told me to be careful died of a heart attack." Raven waved her arms. "This small-town hominess is hiding something evil...or we brought it with us."

"We need to remain vigilant." Buzz tapped the cell phone in his pocket. "I'm expecting an update from Colonel Scripps on the situation in Burumanda. Town by town, the rebel forces are falling. The president should be able to return any day now and take his daughter with him."

A sudden ache flooded Raven's chest. She folded her arms over her stomach. As much as she wanted Malika safe in her own country with her father, she'd miss her...even the sticky hands. And Buzz could believe it or not.

"About that bonfire tonight, Buzz." Raven buttoned her coat against the chill. "I don't think Malika should go."

"I agree, but we're going to have a heck of a time keeping the other two at home, and Malika's been following them around like a shadow." He opened the door of the truck for her and tucked her coat under her leg.

She put out a hand before he could close the door. "Do you still think I'm using Malika to get to you?"

"I guess my plan to make you so mad you'd run

back to New York didn't work, did it? You're not going anywhere, are you? You're not leaving her."

She shook her head. *I'm not leaving you, either.*

Buzz wheeled his truck up the drive of the ranch and pointed to a silver minivan. "Shep's back and he must have the kids with him."

"More kids?" Raven gripped the edge of the leather seat.

Buzz suppressed a smile. Somebody up there was testing Raven. And as far as he could tell, she'd been passing with flying colors. She'd blamed herself for Wyatt getting snatched but nobody else did, not even Josie.

"When Shep has the minivan with him, it means he's come back with a couple of grand-kids in tow."

"I think the decibel level in the house is going to rise even more." She covered her ears and grimaced.

"I think Shep saved us." Buzz threw the truck into Park and stomped on the parking brake. "He just gave us a good reason for staying home from the bonfire."

Before Buzz could get to Raven's door, she'd thrown it open with a little smile twisting her lips. Did she think he was trying to make it up to her after his clumsy effort at getting her out of town?

He could think of a few better ways to make up to her besides opening her car door.

Shep bounded down the front steps with the energy of a man twenty years his junior and crushed Buzz in a big bear hug. "Good to see you home, Buzz. I was hoping it was for good."

"Not yet, Shep. You just waiting to retire?"

"Maybe." His teeth flashed in his brown face as he turned to Raven. "Is this the new Mrs. Buzz I've been hearing about?"

Raven held out a tentative hand as if warding off a bear hug. "I'm Raven. I've heard a lot about you, too."

Shep took her hand in both of his, a light shining from his dark eyes. "That's a real special little girl you've got."

"Thanks, we think so, too."

Pulling Raven's arm through his, Shep called over his shoulder at Buzz. "I brought Alexis and Patrick. Wyatt's happy to have another boy in the house. He's a lot quieter than I remember. Maybe those girls shut him down."

Yeah, or maybe that stranger shut him down.

With the kids playing a noisy board game on the floor of the family room and the adults ensconced in the quieter living room, Buzz broached the idea of staying away from the bonfire.

"After the excitement of today, I think it's a

good idea if the kids stay home." Buzz rolled his shoulders back against the cushion of the sofa, trying to look relaxed. "The bonfire gets wild, anyway, with all the teenagers goofing around."

Josie cupped her wineglass. "Do you really think there's some creep out there preying on little kids? You told me on the phone Sheriff Tallant hadn't heard of any more incidents."

"Not necessarily, but some creep did pick up Wyatt for some reason, and I think Wyatt's spooked."

"I agree, Josie." Austin rubbed his wife's thigh. "Wyatt's been on the quiet side since he got home. We can have our own campfire here and roast marshmallows."

Shep lifted his shoulders. "I don't need to go out tonight after driving all day and the kids are just happy to be out of the car."

Buzz eased a slow breath through his teeth. That was easy enough. If he could keep Malika here on the ranch, he could protect her until President Okeke sent for her.

"Okay, marshmallows at home it is. I need to bake a few pies for Thanksgiving dinner anyway." Josie stretched and held her glass out to Austin. "Can you pour me another half glass? I'm going to need some fortification when I tell the kids no bonfire tonight."

A few hours later, after the kids had happily accepted their fate, they bunched around the counter helping Josie with the pies and making a mess.

Raven sat on the arm of the sofa and nudged Buzz in the back. "She makes it look so easy."

"Josie?" He snorted. "Don't let the Susie Homemaker facade fool you. I've seen her dump the kids' stuff in Austin's lap, grab her keys and announce that she had to leave the house before she committed an act of violence."

"She's got them wrapped around her floursmudged fingers right now." Raven tipped her head toward Josie handing out pecans to the kids.

"Do you think parents are perfect twenty-four/seven? A few slip-ups don't cancel out the overall effect of good parenting."

She leaned her head against his hip. "How'd you get to know so much about parents?"

"I had two good ones." His cell phone in his pocket rang and he dug it out. One glance at the display told him it wasn't the call he'd been waiting for from Colonel Scripps. "Hello?"

"Hey, Buzz. It's Clay Benedict at the airport. There's a problem with your Jetstream—electrical fire. I noticed some smoke coming from the hangar and when I got there, the stuff was pouring out of the wing mechanism."

Buzz's heart stuttered. It had been damage to his airplane that had caused the deaths of his parents. "It was just my plane or was there some kind of fire in the hangar?"

"Just your plane, buddy. Thought you'd want to come and have a look."

"I do. I'll be right there."

Raven hooked a finger in his belt loop. "Something wrong with your plane?"

"Yeah, I'm going to the airport to check it out."

"I'm coming with you." She swept a hand across the scene in the kitchen. "Your sister, Austin, Shep—they have everything under control. I'm feeling useless."

"Okay, I'll grab your coat from the closet."

Raven wedged between the kids at the counter. "Buzz and I are going to the airport to check on his Jetstream. There's some problem."

Ducking into the closet, Buzz pulled his jacket from a hanger, took his weapon from the top shelf and zipped it into his inside pocket. He draped Raven's coat over his arm and waited by the front door.

"We shouldn't be too long, but go ahead with the fire anyway."

On the drive to the airport, Raven asked, "Did the guy at the airport say what was wrong?"

"An electrical fire in the wing mechanism. I didn't do much of an inspection when we landed, but I didn't notice any problems."

When they got to the airport, Clay exited the

small office building to meet them. "I'm real sorry, Buzz. I hope we didn't do anything to cause that damage."

Buzz strode into the hangar, his footsteps echoing in the space. He examined the wing and noticed some damage to the wires underneath the wing flaps. It could've happened during landing.

Clay flicked the scorched wires with his fingers. "I was thinking maybe the mechanism that deploys the flap overheated, but I don't get how that could happen with the bird stationary."

"Maybe the wires were loose and touched off a spark. Do you have any mechanics on duty?"

"Not until after the Thanksgiving weekend, Buzz." Clay smacked the side of the jet. "Are you in a hurry to get out of town?"

"Not now." A vague sense of unease had settled around Buzz like a cloud of noxious air. "Thanks for the heads-up, Clay. Give me a call when your mechanic comes in."

"Will do, Buzz. Good to see you again, Raven."

When they got back into the truck, Buzz leaned on the steering wheel and stared out the windshield. "How the hell did that happen?"

Raven gasped. "You're not suggesting the damage to the plane has anything to do with Malika, are you?"

"I think I am." He pounded the steering wheel. "Even if someone didn't deliberately sabotage my plane, the effect is the same. We can't just take off with Malika now, even if we wanted to."

"We could drive."

"How hard do you think it would be to track us in a car? We don't even know who to look out for. Do you think these guys have signs pasted to their chests that read *terrorist?*"

"I don't know, Buzz. Maybe we're jumping to conclusions. Think about it. Everything that has happened in White Cloud since we arrived has been peripheral to Malika. My near-miss and the rodeo clown had nothing to do with Malika. She wasn't even with me."

"Go on." He had to let her at least try to talk herself out of her fear.

"Maybe it was that guy, Lance Cooper, who's still so upset about his brother. I don't mean he was trying to kill me, but maybe just giving me a scare to get back at you. And the whole thing with Wyatt could have been random."

"And the plane?"

"An accident. Accidents happen all the time." She covered her mouth with her hand. "I'm sorry."

Buzz closed his eyes and tilted back against the headrest. Did it still hurt? Yeah, but not so much since Josie stopped blaming him…and with Raven by his side. He cranked on the engine.

"Since we're here, do you want to drop by the bonfire?"

"Okay, but we'd better not tell the kids."

"My lips are sealed." The truck churned up gravel as he peeled out of the airport parking lot. On the way to the rodeo grounds, he pulled into a grocery store so they could pick up the items Josie had requested before they left.

They walked out of the store, each holding a bag. As they stepped into the parking lot, Buzz nearly dropped his when he saw a man lounging against the hood of his truck. Buzz shoved his bag into Raven's arms. "Stay here."

Feeling for his weapon in his pocket, Buzz stalked across the asphalt. "Get the hell away from my truck."

The man raised a pair of sandy eyebrows and shrugged off the hood. "Little tense, aren't you, Richardson?"

Buzz's nostrils flared and he tucked his hand into his inside pocket. "You'd better start talking and talking fast or you're going to have a .45 resting right between your eyes."

The man clicked his tongue. "The Agency said you were a hothead, had to be to take off with the little girl like that."

"You're with the Agency?" Buzz's fingers curled around the handle of his gun. "Prove it."

He held up his hands and then slipped a finger

beneath the collar of his shirt and drew out a ribbon with a badge dangling from the end. The guy had to be CIA and probably a desk jockey to boot. They were the only ones who wore their badges around their necks.

Buzz inched forward and yanked the badge toward him for a closer look. Jeb Russell. Yeah, it looked legitimate. So the Agency had tracked him down.

"What do you want, Russell? You're not getting the girl. President Okeke and I have an agreement."

The agent's eyes narrowed. "Would that agreement include intel on Jack Coburn...the traitor?"

Buzz lunged at Russell and grabbed the lapels of his cheap jacket. "That's a lie and if you boys would do your jobs instead of kissing diplomatic butt, maybe Prospero wouldn't have to color outside the lines to find Jack."

"Prospero? Really?" Russell pulled away from Buzz's grip and shook out his jacket. "I heard you guys packed it in."

Buzz snorted. "Just like the CIA to have the wrong information."

Russell pointed his finger at Buzz. "You're going to keep that girl in this Podunk backwater town until we release her to her father, and I'm going to make sure of it."

Buzz smacked the finger out of his face as

Raven joined him, jostling the two bags. "Buzz? Is everything okay?"

"The U.N. expand its job duties for translators, Ms. Pierre?" Russell smirked as he turned away and strolled to his car.

Raven's mouth dropped open. "Who was that?"

"CIA." Buzz took a bag from her arms and hit the remote for his truck. "And I think I know who sabotaged the plane."

"That man's a CIA agent? Why would he damage your plane?"

"The Agency wants us to stay here. He's going to be keeping an eye on us to make sure we do."

"Did you tell him? Did you explain to him that Malika's in danger here?"

"I didn't tell him anything, and I don't want you to either, Raven."

She nodded, a stubborn line creeping along her jaw. "He's not going anywhere near Malika."

When they pulled into a parking space near the carnival, Buzz scanned the crowd of people. Was there someone out there waiting for Malika to show up? Was Russell still on their tail?

He couldn't identify one of Farouk's guys on sight. Profiling didn't work for Farouk's group. He'd pulled together a bunch of disgruntled miscreants from all four corners of the globe.

That couple in Colorado who'd been racing former Prospero member Ian to the suitcase packed with a deadly virus had been Russian. Farouk had Germans, Italians and Spaniards working for him. He probably even had a few Americans.

Any one of these people could be Malika's enemy.

Raven snapped down the mirror on the visor and rubbed her lips together to blend her lipstick. "Are we getting out or what?"

Buzz pushed open the door of the truck and sniffed the acrid air. Bits of ash swirled in the wind before settling on the hood of his truck.

Tilting her nose in the air, Raven breathed. "Smells good—like autumn and russet leaves and excitement. Too bad the kids had to miss out."

"Too bad, but—" he twined his fingers through hers "—kind of nice to be alone."

They swung hands as their feet crunched the leaves on the ground. Raven rested her head on his shoulder and he had never felt more right than at this moment in time. He should've married her three years ago and figured out the kid situation later.

"Buzz." Her fingers tightened on his. "You don't really think I'm using Malika to get to you."

"Nah, not any more than I'm using her to get info on Jack. I just wanted to get you out of White Cloud. Still do."

"It's funny when you think about it. You'd

spent a long time trying to get me here, and now you're trying to make me leave."

"Different circumstances." They skirted the edge of the bonfire, its flames leaping into the air. The fire's oranges and reds played across Raven's face, lighting her dark hair with a mysterious glow.

She placed her cool hands on either side of his face. "You look like a satyr with your face in shadow and the fire glowing behind you."

"I was thinking the same thing about you." He turned his head and kissed her palm. When they got Malika back home, they'd have to figure out some way to be together, whether Raven decided to take the leap into parenthood or not.

"Your hands are cold. Let's warm up." He pulled her closer to the bonfire, wedging between the press of people toward the warmth.

The organizers of the event continued to throw kindling into the fire, and some rowdy teenagers decided to add some fuel of their own. Buzz searched the crowd for a police presence. If Sheriff Tallant's deputies were on hand, they weren't visible.

As the fire gobbled up the kindling, it rose to even greater heights, leaping and dancing in wild abandon. The people closest to its warmth began to step back, while the people on the outside of the circle pressed in. Both groups crushed the middle and Buzz clung to Raven's hand.

Buzz shouted. "I think we should get out of here."

She slipped her hand from his to cup her ear. "What? The noise is deafening."

At that moment, the crowd surged forward in one mass and Buzz made a desperate grasp for Raven. Several more people drawn like moths to the ever-burgeoning fire pushed between them. Being taller than everyone in his range, Buzz spotted the top of Raven's head but he couldn't reach her. She continued to bob, adrift in a sea of humanity, squeezing between frantic parents and giddy teens.

Out of the corner of his eye, Buzz saw a hooded figure in dark sunglasses cut a swath through the crowd. Raven lay in the man's direct path. A rush of adrenaline coursed through Buzz's veins and he shouted at Raven. The man continued to make a beeline for her.

Then she slumped into the stranger's arms.

Chapter Fourteen

A bug stung Raven's neck and she reached up to flick it away. But it proved too much work to lift her hand. Her knees buckled and she teetered to the side. A pair of strong arms broke her fall and she collapsed into their embrace.

Buzz? No. This man smelled of fuel and fire and danger.

Raven jerked her head back, arching away from the man's chest. A face swam before her hazy vision. Huge black eyes stared back at her. Bug eyes. The sting. A man with bug eyes. She giggled.

The bug-man supported her wobbly frame and somehow maneuvered through the crowd of people, dragging her along with him. Again, a shot of fear lanced through Raven's body. She bucked and struggled against the force pulling her away...away from Buzz.

A disembodied voice murmured, "A little too much to drink. Overcome by the smoke."

Raven opened her mouth to give voice to the scream clogging her throat, but her jaw hung open uselessly. Her eyelids fluttered and then weights dragged them down and darkness enclosed her. She tried to pump her legs, but her muscles wouldn't respond to her command.

Then she smelled it. Gasoline. Her nostrils flared and she gagged on the fumes. Her wet hair clung to her cheek. Why was she wet? The dampness soaked through the leg of her jeans. Terror flooded her senses and she clawed at her abductor.

The press of bodies around them suddenly disappeared and a cool breeze whipped her face. She mumbled a protest or a thanks. Her sluggish brain couldn't tell the difference and her numb tongue couldn't form the words.

Her attacker dropped her. She struggled to her hands and knees, still blind, and began crawling in the dirt. Twigs and sharp rocks cut into her palms. Then a strong arm hooked beneath her waist, yanking her backward.

A crackling noise, a flash of warmth on her cheek and the smell of burning wood assaulted her senses. She could tell they'd left the confines of the bonfire, but still hot orange flames danced behind her closed lids. Panic forced a cry from her throat and a burst of adrenaline gave her strength.

She twisted away from the arm that imprisoned her and staggered away from the heat of the fire.

Then out of the blackness came a voice. Buzz's voice. "Raven!"

She peeled open one heavy lid just in time to see Buzz fly through the air and tackle a hooded figure, clutching a flaming branch. She choked out a puny scream as the two fell to the ground. The man with the hood lurched to his knees and tossed the branch.

The branch sailed through the air toward Raven as if in slow motion. The smell of the gasoline on her hair and clothing flooded her senses. She crawled an inch, maybe two before the stick of fire landed next to her foot. Encouraged by the fumes, the flame jumped to Raven's pant leg. A searing pain brought a wail of agony to her lips.

Then it was gone. Buzz swooped in and lifted her away from the fire. His heavy jacket covered her leg, smothering the flame.

Raven whimpered while Buzz rocked her gently in his arms, whispering into her hair. "It's okay. I've got you."

Her nightmare had ended and she was safe in Buzz's embrace. She could sleep now.

COTTON FILLED RAVEN'S MOUTH and she smacked her lips against the dryness. Immediately a straw nudged her mouth and Buzz said, "Drink."

Raven sucked on the straw and cool relief flooded her mouth and coursed down her throat. She squeezed her eyes once and then blinked several times. Buzz's face, lined with worry, appeared framed by white hospital walls.

"How are you feeling?"

"Uhh, groggy."

"He drugged you. Then he was going to…" Buzz's jaw clenched and he gripped her hands folded on top of the white hospital sheets.

"Set me on fire." She shivered and touched the bandage on her leg. "How's my leg?"

"Thank God, it's not badly burned. The fire caught on to your jeans just above your boot. The boot didn't burn very quickly." He traced a finger along the edge of the bandage.

"Thanks to you, Buzz. I couldn't function, couldn't get away from the fire." She shook her head, passing a hand across her face. "At least we got him, at least one of them. There may be more."

Buzz jumped up from his chair by the bed and paced to the window. He drew down a slat of the blinds and peered outside. "That's the thing, Raven. I didn't get him. While I was helping you, he escaped."

She covered her hand with her mouth, and then dropped it and smoothed out the covers. "That's all right, Buzz. You saved me. With that gasoline soaking my clothes I would've gone up in flames if you hadn't acted when you did."

"I didn't even get a good look at him. His sunglasses never came off during the struggle. I grabbed his hood, but only managed to twist it over his face. Then when he threw that branch..." He turned away from the window and straddled the chair. "I couldn't lose you, Raven."

She extended her hand and he took it, chaffing it between his two big, warm palms. "I don't understand, Buzz. Malika wasn't even with us. Why is he after me?"

"Maybe just to remove one more layer between him and his target. Maybe to punish you for thwarting his plans. Maybe..." He stopped and his blue eyes gazed at something in the past.

"What? What are you thinking?"

"I didn't tell you this before, Raven, but when I came in to help Ian lift that suitcase from the Rocky Mountains, I shot someone."

"Yeah, well, that happens in your line of work—I mean, in your previous line of work."

"I shot a woman and I heard later she was Farouk's girlfriend."

"So you think...?"

"Farouk obviously knows I'm involved in Malika's protection. Hell, he may even know about my connection to White Cloud. Maybe that's how they found us. He's after you because I killed Katrina, his girlfriend. Revenge."

"Really?" Raven's voice took on an uncharacteristic squeak and she cleared her throat. "Some terrorist looking to take over Burumanda is going to get personal?"

"Farouk's a special case. He and Prospero had almost a cat and mouse game going. He used a lot of intelligence to find out who we were. I wouldn't be surprised if he's behind Jack's disappearance. In fact, I'd bet on it."

"And he wants to kill me to avenge Katrina's death?" Raven's burn, which hadn't been bothering her before, now throbbed beneath the bandage.

"It makes sense. Why else go after you when you don't have Malika?" He smoothed the back of his hand down her cheek. "We need to leave White Cloud and damn the consequences and the CIA."

"Can you get another plane at the airport?"

"Not likely."

She grabbed his wrist. "Buzz, do you think Farouk had someone sabotage your plane? I know you thought it might've been that agent, Russell. But the guy who drugged me smelled like fuel, oil, and I don't think it was from the bonfire."

His eyes narrowed and glittered dangerously from the slits. "Sabotaged the plane?"

The stoniness of his face frightened her and she flinched. Had she suggested something ridiculous? "Y-yes, the plane, so we couldn't get away quickly with Malika."

"Sabotage?" He jerked away from her and buried his face in his hands.

"Buzz? Are you all right? What's the matter?"

He lifted his head and stared at her, his face caged behind his fingers. "My parents. It was Farouk. He saw an opportunity, maybe to kill me, and he damaged my plane that day. Only it wasn't me flying. It was Josh…and my parents."

"No. Buzz, you're jumping to conclusions." Was he going to find another way to blame himself for his parents' deaths?

"I don't think so." He balanced his chin on bunched fists. "I always suspected Farouk had a hand in the blast that killed my Prospero teammate Riley's wife. Who knows what he attempted with Ian? Maybe he's already killed Jack."

She dabbled her fingers along the hard line of his jaw. "The only way you're going to find out for sure is to capture him."

They both jumped when a doctor swung through the door, tapping his clipboard. "I'm Dr. Abbott. How are you doing, Mrs. Richardson?"

She was becoming way too accustomed to that name. "I'm fine, Doctor. How bad is the burn?"

"It's not too bad. We kept you over mostly

for the drugs in your system. Have the police spoken to you yet?" The young doctor adjusted his glasses and threw a nervous glance at Buzz, who still vibrated with pent-up fury.

"Not yet. Have you talked to them, Buzz?" Raven didn't have a clue what story Buzz wanted to put out there.

"I spoke with Sheriff Tallant." Buzz crossed his arms over his impressive chest, almost daring the doctor to probe any further.

Dr. Abbott didn't take the dare. "Well, then, if that's been taken care of, we can release you, Mrs. Richardson. Keep that loose dressing on your leg for the rest of the day or at least until you feel you can prop up your leg and not break or puncture the blisters. Ibuprofen should work for any pain. You were very lucky."

"Very lucky." Raven smiled at Buzz.

When Dr. Abbott left, Raven's smile faded. "How soon can we get out of White Cloud and what mode of transportation are we using?"

"We're going to have to drive…and drive. We can't risk getting on a commercial airline with Malika—too easy to track."

"And a car isn't going to be easy to follow?"

"Let me worry about that. We'll spend Thanksgiving at the ranch tomorrow, and then we take off."

Raven swung her legs over the side of the hospital bed and sat up. "I know what I'm going to be thankful for."

"When this is all over and you're back in Manhattan?"

Raven swallowed and nodded. Being alone in Manhattan was the furthest thing from her mind.

JOSIE SMACKED A PILLOW against her hand and then wedged it beneath Raven's leg propped up on the coffee table. "I can't believe someone pushed you into a fire, Raven. I wouldn't even do that."

"Josie!" Scowling at his wife, Austin drew a finger across his throat.

"I'm just kidding." She patted Raven's shoulder. "Raven knows that by now, don't you, Raven?"

"Yeah, sure, Josie." She grabbed Josie's hand as it rested on her shoulder and squeezed. "Not a word to Malika about anyone pushing me into the fire, right? It was just an accident."

"Yeah, sure, Raven." She glanced at Buzz reading his book. "Not a word to anyone about anything. I know the drill. Can I get you some tea?"

"I can do that. I feel guilty enough already with you preparing everything for the Thanksgiving dinner tomorrow. The doc told me to take it easy, not become an invalid." She reached for the pillow, but Buzz jumped from his chair.

"I'll get you some tea."

Josie snuggled next to her husband on the sofa.

"So Thanksgiving tomorrow and then we take off the next day. The kids want the weekend at home before going back to school on Monday. What are your plans? Going back to Manhattan? Or Buzz's place in Dallas? Where *do* you two live with Malika anyway?"

Buzz handed a warm mug to Raven and rolled his eyes. "We live in Dallas. I thought I told you that. Raven still has her job at the U.N., though."

"Mmm, tough commute, but I suppose when you're married to a pilot..."

"I thought you knew the drill, Josie." Buzz crossed an ankle over his knee. "You ask a lot of questions for someone who knows the drill."

"I know it, Buzz, but I'm sick of it. I breathed a sigh of relief when you took the job as a commercial airline pilot."

"Then you should still be sighing. That's my job."

"Yeah, right. Just keep your job away from my kids." Josie bounded from the sofa and joined the kids upstairs as they got ready for riding.

Austin lifted a shoulder. "Sorry, Buzz. I'll follow her upstairs to make sure there's no steam coming out of her ears."

"She's right, you know." Raven peeked beneath her bandage and decided to rip it off. "Everyone in this house is in danger."

"I didn't invite them. If I had realized we

were heading here during the Harvest Festival, I would've changed direction. Just one more day to get through."

"Where are we going?"

"Take out a map and throw a dart, but we're not going to Dallas. Maybe we should head east. Should you be doing that?" He gestured toward the bandage dangling from her fingertips.

"Dr. Abbott told me it's better if the burn gets some air. The bandage was just to protect the blistering. Pretty, huh?" She wiggled her foot, dropping the bandage to the table.

He captured her foot in his hand and caressed her heel. "Everything about you is pretty."

"Have you developed a foot fetish in my absence?"

Buzz's grin eased some of the tension she'd been feeling since she woke up in a hospital bed that morning. She and Malika would be fine. Buzz would see to that.

"To match your shoe fetish?"

"Hey, give me some credit here. I've been living in those boots all week and now one of them has a big burn mark on it. Do you think Daisy's has another pair?"

"I think you'll be back in New York before you have to buy another pair." Buzz picked up the white bandage from the coffee table and crumpled it in his fist.

Did he care? Raven's gaze tracked over the corded muscles in his forearm and the white knuckles of his hand.

Did she have the guts to care back? Could one week with an adorable little girl really change a lifetime of fear over being a parent? "Buzz..."

The kids tumbled down the stairs, shrieking and laughing. Malika skipped up to Raven. "How is your leg, Mama?"

"It's fine." She pinched Malika's nose. "What has you so excited?"

"Buzz-Daddy is taking us riding." She placed a small hand on Buzz's knee. "If he can leave you."

The delicate features of Malika's face crumpled and Raven leaned forward to clinch her in a hug. They hadn't fooled her. She knew Raven's burn had something to do with their precarious situation.

"Of course, Buzz-Daddy can take you. I'm fine. Go out there and have fun. Are Shep's grandkids joining you?"

Buzz pointed to the window. "They're at his place right now, but they're coming over, too. All the kids are good riders."

Josie hopped off the last step and winked. "At least you have a good excuse for not learning to ride now...and I am kidding. Do you want me or Austin to sit with you while Buzz takes the kids out?"

Raven crinkled her brow. "Buzz is taking the kids out? You mean out of the paddock thingy? I don't think Malika's ready for that."

"No, just my two brats and Shep's. Buzz will stay with Malika in the paddock...thingy." Josie clapped a cowboy hat that came down almost to her nose on her head.

"That's okay. You and Austin came here to enjoy the ranch with your kids. It's not like I can't walk."

In a flurry of hats and boots and giggles, the kids tumbled outside with the adults on their heels.

Raven tipped her head back and closed her eyes. She and Buzz hadn't told Malika they were leaving the ranch. She'd be disappointed, but if anything, Malika had the adaptability of a chameleon. If Josie suspected Malika wasn't who they said she was, it didn't come from Malika's demeanor. She'd played her part of the adopted daughter to perfection.

Too much perfection.

Raven felt so close to Malika, the girl's departure was going to rip her heart out. But that didn't mean she was ready for kids of her own.

Her cell phone vibrated and Raven jumped. Checking the caller ID, she recognized the number as coming from a U.N.-issued cell phone.

Colonel Scripps had contacted her boss, Walter. Was he finally checking in?

"Hello?"

"Hello, Ms. Pierre. This is Agent Russell. We met yesterday in the grocery store parking lot."

Raven pushed up from the sofa and wandered to the window, which framed the kids on their horses. "What do you want?"

"I'd like to have a chat with you. Can you meet me somewhere in town?"

Her breath hitched. "Are you crazy?"

"No, are you? Do you know the penalty for kidnapping, Ms. Pierre?"

"Nobody kidnapped the child." She steadied her grip on her cell phone.

"Oh, has Richardson been spinning some yarn about how he had a secret agreement with President Okeke to take his daughter?"

Raven leaned her forehead against the cold glass of the window. "It's the truth. I was there. We had the full cooperation of the Burumandan security guards."

Russell rasped out a harsh laugh. "Have you been following the news, Ms. Pierre? Have you seen the state of Burumanda lately? How do you know those security guards weren't working against the president?"

"I—I— Buzz wouldn't kidnap a child." Her

world might have been topsy-turvy at the moment, but she knew that as a fact.

He tsked and her blood boiled at his condescending manner.

"I'm not suggesting he wants to harm the girl, but he's using her as a pawn to get information from President Okeke about his Prospero team member Jack Coburn. And we know for certain Coburn's a traitor."

Raven brushed her hair from her face in irritation. "Look, what do you want from me?"

"I want the girl."

"You *are* crazy. Why would I turn her over to you?" Raven laughed even though her stomach churned, and she had to grip the windowsill for support.

"To save Buzz Richardson."

"How is turning President Okeke's daughter over to you going to save Buzz?"

"I told you, Raven." He huffed out a breath as if speaking to a child. "Buzz is wanted for kidnapping. The president wants his daughter back and I'm here to make that happen. You can ensure that things go a lot easier for yourself if you deliver her to me."

"A lot easier for me?" She wanted to end the call but Russell's words held her captive.

"You're an accomplice to the kidnapping.

When Buzz goes down, you're going down with him."

"It's not a kidnapping when you have the father's permission." She stared at Malika on her pony, her pigtails flying behind her as she laughed at Buzz.

"Says you. Did President Okeke tell you personally to take his daughter? Have you had any contact with him since you've been on the run?"

Her silence spoke volumes. She'd never heard President Okeke ask Buzz to abscond with his daughter. Buzz hadn't spoken to the president once since they'd taken Malika. She had only Buzz's word.

Russell whistled. "I thought so. Kidnapping. Bring the girl to me now and we'll let you off the hook completely. You'll be free to go back to Manhattan and put this episode behind you."

Sacrifice Buzz and a child to save herself? This guy had her number. Two years ago, she would've jumped at the chance. Hell, she would've jumped at the chance two weeks ago.

"Remember, Ms. Pierre, Raven, you have no proof that President Okeke gave his permission for Richardson to take the child."

She had only Buzz's word.

The setting sun shot streaks of orange through the cloudy gray sky. Its magnificence silhouetted the figures in the paddock. Buzz lifted Malika off her pony and swung her around, her feet with the red cowboy boots flying through the air.

Buzz's word had always been good enough for her.

"Russell?"

"Yes?"

She could almost picture the slimeball rubbing his hands together. "You and the CIA can shove it."

An hour later, the riders burst through the side door full of their adventures, with Britney and her brother arguing about who rode faster and jumped higher.

Malika's lower lip protruded in a pout and Raven scooped her up and plopped her on top of the counter that separated the kitchen from the family room. She whispered in her native tongue. "What's the matter? You didn't have fun?"

Malika responded. "I had fun, but I want to ride like Wyatt and Britney and the others."

"You're learning so fast, but you're not ready to leave the paddock yet. The other kids have been riding for a long time." She pulled off one of Malika's little red boots. "You will have more time to learn."

Raven caught her breath as she looked into Malika's big brown eyes, liquid with tears. Of course, Malika wouldn't have time to learn. She wasn't going to stay on the ranch forever, and she knew it.

Raven yanked off the other boot and popped up to kiss Malika on her smooth cheek. "Maybe you will continue lessons at home."

"Malika, tell us the word for horse again in your language." Britney turned to her mother. "Malika's been teaching us her language and we've been teaching her—" Wyatt elbowed his sister in the ribs "—other stuff."

Malika smiled and carefully pronounced the word for horse in her dialect, and the other kids repeated it, giggling over the strange sounds.

"That's fantastic." Josie clapped her hands. "Now everyone upstairs for a bath and a quick nap…if you want one. I'm not cooking tonight, so who wants to go into town to pick up pizza? We'll invite Shep and the grandkids, too."

"I'm going to stick by the invalid." Buzz jerked his thumb at Raven.

"And I'm the cook tomorrow, so it looks like it's you, Austin." Josie kissed her husband and herded the kids upstairs.

Raven tagged along after Buzz and when he shut the bedroom door she stretched out on the bed. *Might as well come out with it.*

"Agent Russell called me this afternoon."

Buzz froze midway through pulling off his

boot, and nearly tumbled from the chair face-first. "You're kidding me."

"Would I kid about something like that?" She propped up her head, digging her elbow into the mattress. "He called me on my cell phone. I've gotta change that number. It's become the worst-kept secret in town."

"Don't joke around, Raven. What did he want?"

"Oh, I'm serious. Deadly serious. He wanted me to give up Malika."

Buzz tugged his boot off the rest of the way and dropped it on the floor with a thud. "Why does the CIA want her all of a sudden, and why would Russell think you'd just hand her over?"

"To your first question, I haven't a clue. To the second, he told me I could avoid kidnapping charges if I brought her to him."

"Kidnapping charges? That's a stretch." He started working on his other boot.

"He assured me that you didn't have President Okeke's permission to take Malika."

"But you didn't believe him."

Raven rose from the bed and sat cross-legged on the floor before him, favoring her burned leg. She gripped his boot and pulled. "I believe *you*."

Leaning forward, Buzz kissed the top of her head. He rubbed a strand of her hair between his fingers absently. "I wonder why Russell wants

Malika. The Agency would be thrilled to get its paws on that weapon system."

"The one that can deliver a deadly virus to as many people as possible at one time?" Raven pulled back. "Do you think the CIA would use a child to blackmail President Okeke? They'd be no better than the terrorists."

"Russell could be a rogue agent. It happens." He wedged a finger beneath her chin and tilted it up. "Now we have two reasons to get out of White Cloud—looks like we need to keep Malika safe from Russell, as well."

"I'm ready to leave."

His lips quirked. "Not the best introduction to my home town, was it?"

"Under different circumstances—" Raven placed her hands on his knees and hoisted herself to her feet "—it could've been wonderful."

He traced a finger around the outside of her burn. "How's your leg?"

"Looks better, doesn't it? I'm still taking ibuprofen for the pain, but it's not too bad."

Placing his hands around her waist, Buzz stood up and hugged her close, folding her against his body. "Thanks for believing in me. I've asked a lot of you these past few days, dragged you halfway across the country, put you in danger, foisted a kid on you."

Raven looked into his eyes and placed her

hands on his solid chest. "It's nothing I didn't want to do, Buzz."

And in her heart, Raven could feel the truth of that statement like a warm glow. She'd been living a half-life these past two years without Buzz.

His arms tightened around her. "I believe in you too, Raven. I believe in your commitment to that little girl, and that's enough. Now I'm sure you're sick of hugging this dusty old cowboy, so I'm going to hop in the shower."

Hands on her hips, she watched him peel off the dirty clothes from his magnificent body and disappear into the bathroom with a wink.

She'd never get tired of hugging that man, or kissing him, or touching him, or...

She gave herself a shake and went off to help Malika in the tub.

Later, they gathered in the family room to eat pizza while Josie put the finishing touches on her preparation for the Thanksgiving feast. Some show about the upcoming ball games blared on the TV and Shep had the kids in the corner playing a board game.

Raven reclined on the sofa, her injured leg balanced on Buzz's knee. "So that's it for the Harvest Festival and rodeo?"

"Finished for another year." Austin pulled a slice of pizza from the box and plopped it on his paper plate with one eye on the TV. "With the death of the rodeo clown and Raven's experience with the rowdy teenagers, I'm sure Sheriff Tallant is glad it's over."

"There's always next year." Josie sauntered in from the kitchen, stretched her arms above her head and tousled her hair. "Will you be back next year, Buzz? Or will you…and your family be moving into the ranch?"

"We haven't made any decisions yet, Josie. But I'll tell you what, once we do you'll be the first one we notify."

Josie hissed at him and formed claws with her fingers. "Whatever."

The doorbell rang and Raven involuntarily dug her heel into Buzz's thigh as she threw him a quick glance through widened eyes. "Who can that be on the night before Thanksgiving?"

"I'll get it." Austin struggled to his feet from the floor.

"No." Buzz lifted Raven's leg from his lap and shot to his feet. "I'll answer the door."

Buzz made a stop at the hall closet, and Raven knew he was retrieving his gun. Holding her breath, Raven leaned forward to peer into the foyer. Buzz stood to the side of the door and placed his eye at the peephole.

He called over his shoulder. "It's Sheriff Tallant."

Raven closed her eyes and released a long breath. Buzz had delivered the news for her benefit. Austin and Josie were glued to the TV and Shep was trying to settle an argument over the kids' game.

Maybe the sheriff had some news about the man who had drugged and attacked her. Buzz had convinced the sheriff to keep the details of the crime quiet, but that didn't mean the sheriff and his men weren't keeping an eye on the strangers who still cluttered White Cloud.

Raven eased her legs off the sofa and scooted past Josie and Austin on the floor. She limped toward the hallway, and her gut churned as Sheriff Tallant watched her approach with deep lines engraved on his face.

"What is it? What's wrong?"

Buzz drew her hand through his arm. "I don't know. Sheriff Tallant was just about to tell me. Sheriff?"

Sheriff Tallant shifted from one booted foot to the other. "I'm not sure if this has anything to do with your...accident last night, Raven, but it all seems kind of suspicious. Is your maiden name Pierre?"

"Yes." A cold fear clutched at her heart and she sidled in closer to Buzz.

"We found a dead man tonight…and he had your name and number on a piece of paper crumpled in his fist."

Chapter Fifteen

Raven's body jerked once and slumped against Buzz's. He tightened his arm around her. Maybe they had just gotten lucky. Maybe Russell had taken out the man who had assaulted Raven.

"Was it murder?"

"I'd say a bullet to the back of the head was murder." The sheriff widened his stance and tipped back his hat from his forehead.

Buzz cleared his throat. "Do you have an ID for this man, Sheriff?"

Scratching his chin, Sheriff Tallant said, "That's where it gets hinky, or hinkier. The dead man's a CIA agent—Agent Russell."

Buzz could feel the blood draining from his face and he clenched his jaw. Raven melted into him further as she emitted a small noise from the back of her throat.

Russell had gotten sloppy. In his eagerness to get his hands on Malika, he'd neglected his own safety. If Raven had gone out to meet Russell when he called, she might have met the same fate.

Sheriff Tallant narrowed his faded blue eyes. "Would a CIA agent have any reason to contact you, Raven? Do you know this Agent Russell?"

"I—I…" She pressed against Buzz's side and he could feel her body trembling.

"Yes." Buzz squared his shoulders and tilted his chin. "Agent Russell was here to ask Raven some questions."

"Is this connected to the fire, Buzz?"

"We don't know, Sheriff."

"Hi, Doug. What's going on? Did you find the kids who started that second fire?" Josie shuffled into the hallway, big bunny slippers on her feet.

Sheriff Tallant glared at Buzz from under his shaggy gray brows. "Not yet, Josie. Just wrapping up some business."

Buzz nodded at the sheriff in acknowledgment of his discretion. He stuck out his hand. "We'll keep in touch after we leave, Sheriff."

"Do you want some pie, Doug?" Josie waved her arm behind. "Austin's already started digging into one even though I told him to save it for tomorrow."

"That's okay, sweetheart. Linda's got plenty of pie at home."

"All right, then. Happy Thanksgiving." Josie

swung around, yelling, "Don't you give the kids any of that pie, Austin."

Sheriff Tallant put his hand on the doorknob and turned to the side. "One more thing, Buzz. When I called the Agency to report the murder of Agent Russell, the guy on the phone told me Agent Russell wasn't on any official case for them. He was on vacation. Now why do you suppose he was vacationing in White Cloud?"

Buzz lifted a stiff shoulder. "Maybe he likes rodeos."

When the door slammed behind the sheriff, Raven clutched his arm with cold fingers. "What does it mean, Buzz? Why was Russell killed and what was he doing here in the first place?"

He clasped her hands and tried to rub some warmth into them. "I'm not sure. Obviously, the man who's been after you killed Russell. Maybe the CIA didn't want to tell Sheriff Tallant what their agent was doing here any more than we want to tell him why we're here. Or maybe…"

"Russell was working on his own." She loosened her hands from his and pushed her hair from her face. "I knew it. Russell wanted Malika for himself, not the Agency. He probably wanted to strike a deal of his own. Maybe he was even working with Farouk and was murdered because he strayed from the path. You said he might be a rogue agent."

"It could be, Raven. I'm not going to be so quick to point the finger at a CIA agent. Most of those people I know work hard and are committed to justice."

She shivered. "One more day. We eat turkey and then we trot on out of here."

BUZZ ROLLED TO THE SIDE and nuzzled Raven's neck. She smelled sweet and musky and he wanted to wake up next to her every day for the rest of his life.

They'd made love in the night—slowly, sweetly, tenderly. He'd wanted to ravish her, claim her as his own as they moved along this path of uncertainty. But she'd needed comfort, security... love.

And he had that...in aces. Could she return it this time? Could she return it without worrying about living up to some family ideal that he'd come to realize he had forced on her before?

She opened one sleepy eye, and he kissed her soft lips. "Happy Thanksgiving."

Her lashes fluttered as she untangled her legs from his and stretched her long limbs toward the foot of the bed. "It's going to be good, isn't it, Buzz?"

"Yeah, all good, babe. We'll hightail it out of White Cloud tomorrow with Malika. I'll rent a plane somewhere and we'll take off for a safer place."

She smoothed her hands across his stubble. "I didn't mean all that. I meant Thanksgiving would be good. Kids, family, good home-cooked food."

He grinned as his heart ached for the lost little girl who wanted what she thought she could never have, didn't deserve to have. "That too."

Someone banged on the bedroom door, and Raven clung to him. Was he ever going to get her off this precipice of danger?

"Yeah?"

"Are you decent?" Josie inched open the door and stuck her head through the crack.

"You didn't wait for an answer."

Josie jerked her thumb over her shoulder. "I have jobs for everyone in the kitchen, even the kids. I'm using riding as an incentive for getting the chores done. Shep promised he'd take them out once more before dinner. Malika insisted. That girl is turning into a good little rider already."

"You missed your calling, Josie. You should've been a drill sergeant." Buzz tossed a pillow at the door and Josie slammed it with a huff.

"Do you think Malika will be safe out there with Shep?"

"I'll go out with them, too. I always have

my weapon with me. Nobody is going to get to Malika while I'm there."

She kissed his chin. "I know that, Buzz. Now we'd better shower, dress and report for duty."

Twenty minutes later, Buzz jogged down the stairs. The smells coming from the kitchen made his mouth water. He hadn't had a traditional Thanksgiving dinner since his parents died. At least one good thing had come from his journey to White Cloud—he'd reconnected with Josie.

Josie shoved a pot of potatoes against his chest as soon as he walked into the kitchen. "Peel these. Is Raven coming down or is she shirking her Thanksgiving responsibilities?"

"She's on her way, boss."

"You know, she's kind of grown on me." She elbowed him in the ribs. "And she's a good mom to Malika."

Yeah, she was. A good mom.

When Raven joined them in the kitchen, she surveyed the scene with wide eyes. "There's so much food."

"That's why we're just having bagels for breakfast." Josie waved a knife at a plate of bagels and a tub of cream cheese. "Help yourself and then I've got a job for you."

"I'll bet you do." She scooted next to Buzz at the sink. "You're peeling potatoes?"

"It's my job, and don't distract me or I'm going to peel my finger."

After everyone had eaten breakfast, and the turkey was in the oven, the kids begged to go riding.

Shep pushed to his feet, his gaze still lingering on the football game on TV. "Okay, but Malika's gotta stay in the paddock, and I don't want the rest of you going so far we have to fetch you for dinner or we're going to leave you out there."

Raven shifted a glance toward Buzz and he felt it like a needle. "I'll go out with you, Shep. Then you can go with the kids if they want to take a short ride. I don't think they should be out on their own...not on Thanksgiving."

"Thanks, Buzz."

Josie yawned. "I'm going to take a nap for an hour."

Austin gestured to the TV. "Want to watch the rest of the game with me, Raven?"

Raven agreed to sit through the game with Austin, and a smile tugged at Buzz's lips. She really wanted the full Thanksgiving experience.

He trudged out to the stable with Shep, the kids dancing around them. The excitement of the festival and the Thanksgiving holiday had given all the kids an extra dose of energy. They all seemed switched into overdrive, the air around them buzzing with electricity.

The kids knew enough to saddle their own horses, and he and Shep supervised and secured. Did Malika know it was her last day with Star? It seemed so as she leaned forward and whispered to the pony in her own language. Great, now Star would only understand commands in Chichewa.

The air outside was heavy and Buzz inspected the leaden sky. The wind carried a whiff of rain and a hint of doom.

Buzz shook it off. The imminence of their departure was heightening his sensitivity. Everything had an air of finality because they were leaving the ranch tomorrow.

Shep unlatched the gate to the paddock, and the kids filed in on their horses. The others were a big help to Malika. They were anxious for her to join them on a real ride. Unfortunately for all of them, that was never going to happen.

The horses plodded around the circular paddock until the older kids spurred theirs on to a trot. Shep clapped his hands. "Okay, let's go for a short ride, but we need to be back and cleaned up for Josie's dinner or she'll have my hide."

The kids giggled, and Buzz gripped Star's reins as Malika turned the pony toward the gate that led from the paddock to a tree-lined riding trail. "We'll put Star into a trot, give him a workout. What do you think, darlin'?"

She bestowed a dazzling smile on him. "That is good, Buzz-Daddy."

That was easy. Buzz puffed out a sigh of relief. He really didn't feel like arguing with a five-year-old.

As he watched the last tail flick through the gate, a chill seized him. "Be careful, Shep. Watch the kids."

Shep twisted his body in the saddle and patted the breast of his jacket.

Shep must be armed, too. Had he picked up on Buzz's tension? How could he have missed it? Every fiber in Buzz's body seemed taut and his jaw ached with the stress.

He forced his face into a smile. "Okay, let's see what this pony can do."

Malika contentedly put Star through his paces around the paddock. She had a real connection with the pony, and he seemed happy to do Malika's bidding. Malika had never shown one ounce of fear with Star, and the pony knew he could trust his rider.

He had wanted to get Raven on a horse, but he knew she was afraid. Maybe she could work up to it. Buzz snorted at his hazy dreams of a life with Raven. They hadn't decided anything yet. As far as he knew, she planned to go back to her life in Manhattan when this was all over.

And he planned to find Jack once President

Okeke told him what he knew about Jack's disappearance.

The sky darkened and a fat raindrop splashed on the toe of Buzz's boot. His gaze darted toward the shaded entrance to the riding trail. The damned thing was too dark. He'd have Shep hire someone to clear the heavy foliage from the beginning of that path.

A distant squeal sent Buzz's heart slamming against his chest and he squinted at the trail. A scream jolted him from his boot tips to his head and he strode toward the gate.

"Settle down. Slow down. We're coming to the end." Shep's calming voice washed over Buzz like a dose of tranquilizer, and he closed his eyes and breathed deeply through his nose.

The riders drew up to the gate with Shep's grandson in the lead. Malika trotted over to them eagerly, almost as at ease in the saddle as the rest of the kids.

Shep glanced at the sky. "Looks like a downpour is coming."

"Grandpa, we can still ride horses in the rain, can't we?"

"Sure you can. Horses like the rain, but my old bones don't and I can hear a turkey calling my name."

The kids gobbled all the way to the stables and Buzz and Shep allowed them to unsaddle the horses and put away their gear. Buzz hung on the stable door and stared at the black clouds gathering on the horizon. He couldn't shake the feeling that a dark menace lurked in those clouds.

Raven must have been drinking the same Kool-Aid. When they walked through the side door, she tossed aside a magazine and searched his face. "Everything go okay?"

He took off his hat and hung it on the hook. "Everything went fine. Malika's becoming a fine horsewoman. Shep took the others on a ride up the trail."

Raven shifted her gaze to Malika, shrugging out of her jacket. "Did you have fun, Malika?"

Malika smiled. "Yes, Mama. I had fun."

She clutched her jacket to her chest and scrambled upstairs after the other kids.

"Is it raining yet?" Biting her lip, Raven ducked her head to look out the window.

"Not yet." Buzz came up behind her and massaged her rigid shoulders. "But a storm's on the way. And it's a big one."

RAVEN PATTED HER BELLY after she popped the last forkful of pumpkin pie into her mouth. She might have to buy a whole new wardrobe at Daisy's after this stint in White Cloud. "That was yummy."

Buzz reached over and touched a finger to the

corner of her mouth. "Whipped cream. You were shoveling it in so fast, you missed."

She smacked his thigh and giggled. Really, what had she been so worried about before? A sense of impending calamity had hung over her head the entire time Buzz and Shep had the kids out riding. Must be the weather. The sky was still threatening, but it was teasing them. It wasn't ready to unleash its deluge yet.

Malika sat at Raven's feet, scooping all the whipped cream off her pie. She rested her head against Raven's leg. "Horses like rain, Mama."

"Do they? Don't drop that whipped cream on the floor." She shoved Malika's napkin toward her on the coffee table. "And how about you? Do you like rain?"

"Yes, just like Star."

Raven felt a tightness in her throat. Malika was going to miss that pony. Raven and Buzz planned to tell Malika tonight about their departure tomorrow. Austin and Josie were leaving first thing in the morning, and she and Buzz would be right behind them. Different direction.

A snore drifted from the other sofa, and Josie rolled her eyes. "That's my husband on Thanksgiving—OD'd on football, stuffing and pie.

Shep carried his coffee cup and plate to the kitchen. "Thanks for the hospitality, folks. I think we'll head back to the house."

"But Grandpa, we're going to play Xbox in Wyatt's room."

Josie shrugged. "If that's okay with you, Shep. We let Wyatt bring his Xbox to connect to the TV upstairs and told the kids they could play after dinner."

"If it's okay for you to have a few extra kids on your hands. I think I'm going to go home and follow Austin's example."

"It's fine. Walk carefully." Josie snorted at her own joke.

The kids scurried off to Wyatt's room and the sound of lasers and blasts wafted downstairs.

Josie adjusted Austin's head in her lap and hit the remote on the TV. "I hope you don't mind, Raven. The games aren't too violent, mostly space aliens and that kind of thing. Shut the door, Wyatt."

The sound of alien weapons was muted with the click of the door.

"Do you two want to watch a movie?" Josie aimed the remote at the TV. "There are usually some good classic movies and musicals on for Thanksgiving."

Buzz grunted and opened his newspaper. "Just what I want to watch, a musical."

"Whatever you want, Josie." Raven jumped up to collect the rest of the pie plates and coffee cups. When she settled back on the sofa next to

Buzz, he nudged her leg and tapped the newspaper.

She followed his finger on the newsprint to a black headline: New Burumandan Government Quashes Rebel Forces.

The nightmare was almost over. But had it really been a nightmare? It had brought her and Buzz back together, and she wanted to keep it that way…just as soon as she told him. And it had brought Malika into her life.

Raven smiled and settled back to watch Dorothy. *There's no place like home.*

As the movie neared its conclusion, spatters of rain hit the window. "Rain's finally here."

"Mmm?" Buzz had switched from newspaper to book and rubbed her thigh absently.

Austin still lay sleeping, his head resting in his wife's lap, and Josie had joined him in slumber land, her head tilted back against the cushions of the sofa, her mouth slightly ajar.

Warm domesticity.

"What did you say, babe?" Buzz rubbed his eyes and rested his book on his chest.

"The rain, it's coming."

"I hope the storm spends itself tonight so we don't have a tough drive tomorrow morning."

"We'll tell Malika tonight before she goes to bed, right?"

"Yes, and we can give her some good news too

about her country. We should be able to reunite her with her father any day now."

"Who's going to give you the word?"

"Colonel Scripps."

"I'm going to get some water and check on the kids. They've been destroying aliens for over an hour." Raven strolled into the kitchen and poured herself a glass of water. A low rumble of thunder drew her to the window. Her hands tightened around the glass. "Buzz? Did you and Shep leave the gate to the riding trail open? It looks open."

"No. We always leave that closed. Maybe the wind blew it open."

The sky clapped with thunder again and Raven sloshed water over her hand. A tight knot was forming in her belly. "It's really not that windy."

Suddenly, a streak of blue appeared at the gate. Britney's jacket flew out behind her as she rode her horse into the paddock from the trail. Raven couldn't make out her face, but her actions were jerky, frantic.

Raven dropped the glass where it crashed to the floor. "The kids are outside."

"What?" Buzz bounded to his feet and crowded her at the window.

By this time Britney had been joined by her brother and Shep's two grandkids. All rode their horses into the paddock and slid and tumbled to the ground.

No Malika.

Raven cried out. "Malika's not with them!"

Buzz charged to the closet and grabbed his gun. Then he flung open the side door. Raven forced her rubbery legs to move and followed him outside where the rain pelted her face in angry bursts.

The kids, their faces streaked with tears and mud, left their horses in the paddock and clambered through the gate. "Uncle Buzz, Uncle Buzz. The clown has Malika."

Raven shoved a fist against her mouth to trap the wail that threatened to consume her.

Buzz grabbed Britney's shoulders. "What are you talking about? Where is she?"

"We wanted to take her riding on the trail, Uncle Buzz. She said it was her last day here. She was ready."

"Stop." He held up his hands and Raven marveled at their steadiness. "Where is she? Where did the clown grab her?"

Clown? Raven's mind moved sluggishly.

"He jumped in front of us where the trail bends near that clump of juniper. He must've been hiding in there."

Austin and Josie came running from the house, their faces white with shock. "What happened?"

"Someone has kidnapped Malika." Josie

flinched from the fury in her brother's blue eyes, but it acted like a slap in the face to Raven.

Someone had her little girl. And she was going to get her back.

"We're sorry, Uncle Buzz. We just wanted her to ride like us."

"You said it was a clown, Britney. Was he on a horse?"

"No horse. He was like one of those rodeo clowns. His face was white and he had a red nose and red hair."

Oh dear God. Raven grabbed her upper arms. Was that how he'd been able to blend in all this time?

"Josie, get the kids in the house and call 911. Raven, go with her."

"The hell I will."

Buzz reacted with a slight hitch in his step, but he continued his march into the paddock. "I'm going after him on a horse, Raven. You'll never keep up on foot."

She straightened her spine. "Get me on one of those things. I'm coming with you."

"I'm not putting you in danger. We're just wasting time now."

"You're right. You go ahead and I'll figure out how to climb into one of these saddles on my own."

"You'll kill yourself."

"That's my girl out there."

Buzz swore, but he called over a horse and hoisted Raven into the saddle. "Follow me and just sit there and hold the reins. This horse knows the trail."

Raven's terror at sitting astride the big beast didn't come close to her terror at losing Malika. The horse jolted Raven's spine as he clopped after Buzz's horse and Raven clamped her legs to the animal's sides. Like a mantra, she repeated in her head *he won't harm her, he won't harm her.*

Farouk and his minions needed Malika alive to blackmail President Okeke. They wouldn't hurt Malika. She, on the other hand, was completely expendable. She gritted her teeth and hung on as her horse broke into a gallop to keep up with Buzz's horse. She might be expendable, but she'd give her life to keep Malika safe from harm.

Buzz hunched forward in his saddle. Then he turned and held out a hand. "Pull back on the reins."

Raven tugged, but the horse kept moving forward. She yanked harder, bringing the horse's head up. She didn't know if it was her skillful handling of the reins or peer pressure, but her horse slowed to a stop before it barreled into the back end of Buzz's horse.

Buzz slid from the back of his horse and held a finger to his lips. He hitched the reins over the nearest bush and backtracked to help Raven from her horse.

"Are you okay? You did great."

"I'm fine. Why are we stopping here?"

"This trail comes out almost to the road, running parallel to it. He's been on foot all this time, but he probably has a vehicle waiting for him on the road."

Panic surged from Raven's gut, leaving the bitter taste of bile in her mouth. "Oh my God, once he gets her in the car, she's gone."

"We're not going to allow that. The kids said he didn't have a horse, and Malika's pony wandered back to the paddock. They're on foot and we just made up a great deal of ground. We can't thunder in on a couple of horses. We have to take him by surprise."

"How?"

He tugged her hand. "We're getting off the trail and taking a shortcut. We should be able to see them and reach them before they hit the road and escape."

Buzz swept a branch out of the way, and Raven ducked beneath it, landing in a tangled web of bushes and trees. She'd never imagined the vegetation lining this trail was so lush. It looked like a greenish-brown strip from the house, but many of the bushes had refused to shed their foliage in the fall. And now they offered cover.

After several minutes of creeping quickly through this parallel world, Buzz held out his hand and cocked his head to the side.

Crunching rock and snapping twigs caused Raven's heart to skip a beat. It had to be the kidnapper. The noises ceased and Raven and Buzz froze in midstep.

Thunder boomed above them and a sheet of lightning brightened the clouds in a flash. They used the noise to claw their way to the edge of the riding trail.

A man in the middle of the trail, dark hair sticking out in all directions and white makeup smearing his face, struggled with his burden. *Malika.*

Raven clamped a hand over her mouth to keep from crying out at the sight of Malika's limp form draped over the man's shoulder. He must've drugged Malika the same way he'd drugged Raven the night of the bonfire.

The thunder resounded like a bass drum, and Raven turned wide eyes to Buzz. He had his weapon clutched in front of him, but the man on the trail had his own gun out and he held it perilously close to Malika's head. In desperation, the man might shoot Malika. He'd never give her up willingly.

If only the man were distracted. Buzz could

get a clear shot at him if the kidnapper's gun was pointing away from Malika.

Like a lioness protecting her cub, Raven's instincts shifted into gear and overruled her reason. She crashed through the bushes ahead of Buzz and staggered onto the trail in front of the man holding Malika like a sack of potatoes.

She growled, "You're not taking her anywhere."

The man stumbled in his surprise, his head whipping from side to side, looking for additional people emerging from the bushes. Nobody came. Buzz kept his cover.

He hoisted Malika. "I have my orders. I knew you'd be trouble."

"You're right. I'm trouble. Is that why you tried to take me out? First with the crane and then at the bonfire?"

He licked his lips, lifting his weapon halfway between Malika and Raven. "It was a benefit, but that's not why. I had my orders when it came to you—kill Buzz Richardson's woman, just like we killed his parents."

A cold bead of sweat trickled down Raven's back. Buzz had been right. Farouk had wanted revenge.

He waved the gun. "That rodeo clown saw me swing the crane at you. I had to take him out. Then I picked up the wrong kid at the parade.

Nothing but trouble. Farouk should've handled you himself."

"Well, here I am." Raven spread her arms wide. If he pointed the gun at her, Buzz would have a chance to take him down without harming Malika. Maybe he wouldn't even have time to get a shot off.

The thunder clapped and simultaneously, the skies opened and rain gushed down on them. For just an instant, the man glanced upward and that was all Raven needed. She crouched forward and charged at the man's legs.

He grunted in surprise when she barreled into his kneecaps. He staggered and swung down the hand clutching the weapon. As he did so, an inert Malika slipped from his grasp.

Raven rolled to the side to break Malika's fall when a crack split the air. The man dropped to his knees. The smell of gunpowder stung her nose, and when Malika landed on Raven's back, Raven rolled to cover the girl's body with her own. Another bullet slammed into the man's body and he fell face-forward into the mud on the trail.

"Raven!" Buzz dashed to her side and dropped to the ground. "My God, are you okay? Is Malika okay?"

"I'm fine. Malika is drugged, but she's breathing steadily." Raven rolled off Malika's body and scooped the little girl into her lap. "He almost had her. He almost took her away from me."

Buzz wrapped his arms around both of them from behind. "When you went crashing through the bushes and into the trail, I almost had a heart attack. You're crazy. You took a huge risk."

Raven dashed the tears from her face. "I had to."

A siren blared in the distance, and Raven sniffled and wiped her nose on her rain-soaked sleeve. "Better late than never."

"You're better late than never, Raven Pierre, and I'll wait for you for as long as it takes."

"How about two seconds?" She flung her free arm around his neck and kissed him through her tears and laughter. "I love you, Bryan Richardson, and if you'll take me back we can have ten kids."

"I'll take you back, but there are no conditions to my love, Raven. There are no rules—" he placed a hand on Malika's head "—that define a family except love."

Raven sighed, wrapped in love and content to wallow in the mud with her family.

Two weeks later, Buzz and Raven sat in the backseat of a Lincoln Town Car. Josie and her family had made it home safely. Buzz had told his sister just enough for her to realize Malika was not his adopted daughter and Raven was not his wife. *Not yet.*

Buzz peered out the tinted windows and leaned forward in his seat. "They're here."

Raven scooted next to him and they watched out the window as President Okeke climbed from a limo and Malika trailed after him.

Raven sucked in a breath and Buzz patted her hand. It had been tough for her to part with Malika over a week ago when the CIA had re-united her with her grateful father. And it wouldn't be any easier now.

Buzz speed-dialed Colonel Scripps. "President Okeke is about to board. I'll call you as soon as our meeting is over."

"Find out what you can, Buzz. The Agency is telling me Jack's dead."

Buzz ended the call and worry gnawed at his gut as he pressed his forehead against the car window.

A cool hand caressed the back of his neck and Raven kissed his tense jaw. "Whatever news President Okeke has about Jack, I'm right here with you, Buzz."

The president and his daughter ascended the steps of the private jet and Buzz pushed open the door of the Town Car. "It's showtime."

Lacing his fingers through Raven's, he pulled her across the tarmac to the waiting plane. A few suits—CIA or the Dignitary Protection Division—moved in front of them, but the Burumandan bodyguards waved them up the stairs.

Buzz ducked through the hatch and extended his hand to President Okeke, already strapped in his seat. "Mr. President."

"Mr. Richardson, I can't thank you enough."

Raven had rushed to Malika's side and the two were locked in a big hug, their tears mingling.

"You'll have to allow those two a visit or two… or ten."

The president chuckled. "And thanks to you, I'm going to have to buy my daughter a horse and engage a riding instructor."

"Your daughter could teach that riding instructor a thing or two about horses, sir. I congratulate you on your young country's success in avoiding revolution."

"Yes, my country is safe once again, and we will be more than willing to work with your country in regard to this terrible weapon we possess. No country should have this technology."

"I agree with you, Mr. President. Now, if you'll excuse my frankness, sir, a deal is a deal."

Raven jerked her head up, eyes wide. She kissed Malika on the cheek and joined Buzz, sliding her hand down his back.

The president flashed a wide smile in his

brown face. "I retract my earlier statement, Mr. Richardson. I guess I *can* thank you enough."

"It's all I ask in payment for keeping Malika safe."

President Okeke nodded and crooked his finger. Buzz and Raven hunched forward, and Buzz's breath caught in his throat. Would they finally get something on Jack?

President Okeke whispered in a hushed voice. "He escaped his captors. Nobody knows how and nobody knows where...but Jack Coburn is alive."

Epilogue

Smoothing a hand over his fake moustache, Jack eyed the machine-gun-toting Bundespolizei as they strolled through the Frankfurt airport. He had completed the first leg of his journey successfully. Using the money and resources from the black duffel bag, he'd slapped on a new identity and escaped Afghanistan. He'd rewarded Yasir handsomely on his way out, too. The boy had proved to be an invaluable resource.

Of course, assuming a new identity had been easy since he didn't have a clue about the old one. No, not true. He was Jack Coburn, American spy.

A bead of sweat rolled along the edge of the uncomfortable wig and he nudged the duffel bag farther under the plastic seat with his foot. Since the bag contained stacks of cash and assorted passports, he'd checked it instead of carrying it on and subjecting it to the X-ray machines. He wouldn't have gotten two feet past security with that stash.

Now before he checked it again for the second and final leg of his journey, he'd dip into its contents once more. He figured any good spy worth his salt would switch identities halfway to his destination, and it just so happened his lucky duffel contained another American passport.

Two Bundespolizei sauntered past the self-serve café, and Jack dipped his head to take another bite of his sandwich. He watched them turn the corner through the plain lenses of the glasses perched on the end of his nose and blew out a long breath. He wiped his moustache with a napkin and then dropped it onto the tray.

Easing to his feet, he snagged the strap of the bag and hitched it over his shoulder. Then he grabbed the tray and dumped the remains of his lunch into the trash.

Locating a men's room in a sparsely traveled corridor of the airport, he slipped inside, the duffel banging against his hip. Forty minutes later he slipped out again, a changed man.

He bought his one-way ticket to Miami with cash and hoped the combination of a one-way ticket and cash wouldn't trigger a lookup on some terrorist watch list. He checked the bag again and bought another bag that he stuffed with books and a couple of airport T-shirts, so he'd have something to carry on.

He shuffled through security without a hitch

and strolled to the edge of the screening area to put on his shoes and jacket. Leaning forward, he caught sight of a computer screen on one of the lecterns stationed at the end of the security area. His pulse raced and his gut tightened.

He recognized the face on the screen with an obvious warning message flashing above it. It was the face that had stared back at him from the cloudy mirror in the little shack in Afghanistan.

Jack Coburn was a wanted man.

* * * * *

LARGER-PRINT BOOKS!
GET 2 FREE LARGER-PRINT NOVELS PLUS
2 FREE GIFTS!

♦ Harlequin®

INTRIGUE®

BREATHTAKING ROMANTIC SUSPENSE

YES! Please send me 2 FREE LARGER-PRINT Harlequin Intrigue® novels and my 2 FREE gifts (gifts are worth about $10). After receiving them, if I don't wish to receive any more books, I can return the shipping statement marked "cancel." If I don't cancel, I will receive 6 brand-new novels every month and be billed just $5.24 per book in the U.S. or $5.99 per book in Canada. That's a saving of at least 13% off the cover price! It's quite a bargain! Shipping and handling is just 50¢ per book in the U.S. and 75¢ per book in Canada.* I understand that accepting the 2 free books and gifts places me under no obligation to buy anything. I can always return a shipment and cancel at any time. Even if I never buy another book, the two free books and gifts are mine to keep forever.

199/399 HDN FERE

Name	(PLEASE PRINT)

Address	Apt. #

City	State/Prov.	Zip/Postal Code

Signature (if under 18, a parent or guardian must sign)

Mail to the **Reader Service:**
IN U.S.A.: P.O. Box 1867, Buffalo, NY 14240-1867
IN CANADA: P.O. Box 609, Fort Erie, Ontario L2A 5X3
Not valid for current subscribers to Harlequin Intrigue Larger-Print books.

**Are you a subscriber to Harlequin Intrigue books
and want to receive the larger-print edition?
Call 1-800-873-8635 today or visit www.ReaderService.com.**

* Terms and prices subject to change without notice. Prices do not include applicable taxes. Sales tax applicable in N.Y. Canadian residents will be charged applicable taxes. Offer not valid in Quebec. This offer is limited to one order per household. All orders subject to credit approval. Credit or debit balances in a customer's account(s) may be offset by any other outstanding balance owed by or to the customer. Please allow 4 to 6 weeks for delivery. Offer available while quantities last.

Your Privacy—The Reader Service is committed to protecting your privacy. Our Privacy Policy is available online at www.ReaderService.com or upon request from the Reader Service.

We make a portion of our mailing list available to reputable third parties that offer products we believe may interest you. If you prefer that we not exchange your name with third parties, or if you wish to clarify or modify your communication preferences, please visit us at www.ReaderService.com/consumerschoice or write to us at Reader Service Preference Service, P.O. Box 9062, Buffalo, NY 14269. Include your complete name and address.

HILP11B